Slouching Towards Bethlehem: Wormwood Goes Online

A Modern Spin on *The Screwtape Letters*

R. L. Thorne Cramer

HOLY. BOLD. PUBLISHING
HORSESHOE BEND, IDAHO

The Scriptures marked (KJV) are taken from the King James Bible. Public Domain.

All Scripture quotations marked (NIV) are taken from the Holy Bible, New International Version®, NIV®. Copyright ©1973, 1978, 1984, 2011 by Biblica, Inc.™ Used by permission of Zondervan. All rights reserved worldwide.
www.zondervan.com
The "NIV" and "New International Version" are trademarks registered in the United States Patent and Trademark Office by Biblica, Inc.™

Scripture quotations marked (NLT) are taken from the Holy Bible, New Living Translation, copyright © 1996, 2004, 2007 by Tyndale House Foundation.
Used by permission of Tyndale House Publishers, Inc., Carol Stream, Illinois 60188.
All rights reserved.

Copyright © 2017 Holy. Bold. Publishing.
All rights reserved.

ISBN-13:9781975630898
ISBN-10:1975630890

Dedication

To C. S. Lewis, who showed me that theology and satire can create a powerful music that desires greatly to be sung.

To my husband, Clayton E. Cramer, whose infinite patience always makes my book projects possible.

To my precious Lord Jesus, Whose inspiration never ceases to amaze me.

The Second Coming by William Butler Yeats

Turning and turning in the widening gyre
The falcon cannot hear the falconer;
Things fall apart; the centre cannot hold;
Mere anarchy is loosed upon the world,
The blood-dimmed tide is loosed, and everywhere
The ceremony of innocence is drowned;
The best lack all conviction, while the worst
Are full of passionate intensity.

Surely some revelation is at hand;
Surely the Second Coming is at hand.
The Second Coming! Hardly are those words out
When a vast image out of *Spiritus Mundi*
Troubles my sight: somewhere in sands of the desert
A shape with lion body and the head of a man,
A gaze blank and pitiless as the sun,
Is moving its slow thighs, while all about it
Reel shadows of the indignant desert birds.
The darkness drops again; but now I know
That twenty centuries of stony sleep
Were vexed to nightmare by a rocking cradle,
And what rough beast, its hour come round at last,
Slouches towards Bethlehem to be born?

Preface

I read *The Screwtape Letters* many years ago, and thought C. S. Lewis nailed his generational concerns with a delightful spin. His book chronicles the interaction between two demons, one old and one young, through a series of letters. The older one, Screwtape, mentors the younger one, Wormwood, on how best to go about doing Satan's work.

Christians in every generation have felt the conflict between the Kingdom of God and the Kingdom of Darkness. Many Christians have met the challenge with the power of God and with compassion. Other Christians were overwhelmed. Still others questioned their faith and some even questioned the Faith itself.

Today, it is no different. We have a deep sense of urgency as we look out on a world that is spiraling faster and faster down into chaos. The problems are intensifying with each passing decade. Many countries are embroiled in war. Unrelenting poverty stalks many countries. Disease carries many away, especially the young. Those who follow Jesus are being persecuted. Militant terrorists see death and destruction as perfectly acceptable expressions of their faith. The exploitation and loss of innocent life staggers our imagination.

Many Christians today wish to live a life with Christ at the center. They eagerly want to "fight the good fight" not only to make a difference now, but to leave a legacy of holiness to those who come after them.

But what do we base this holinees on if God's Word is being cast aside for what is seen as a more modern approach to life's challenges?

This book comes from my deep concern for the challenges facing this generation. Using satire as a way of confronting those challenges may seem a bit odd, but C. S. Lewis showed the way. Satire, with its biting humor, is fun to read. Yet, beneath the laughter, it is very confrontational. The humor is a thin veneer for such vexing questions as: "How did we get here? How are we going to fix what confronts United States?"

Today's readers can find many fine books by Christian writers about what is being called "The Culture War." Through research and insightful analysis, minds far greater than mine are pondering solutions.

This book joins that parade, but with a different beat. We explore our modern world through the voices of those causing the havoc. C. S. Lewis' demon, Wormwood, again makes his appearance, as well as his new mentor that I created, Baal-Kobalt. Through them I present the fight we now face: the marginalization of Christianity in the United States and the failure of the Christian church to meet the culture head on.

Of course, many sincere Christians are out on the front lines as dedicated soldiers. But if we are to win this cultural war, we need to better understand the tactics of the enemy and his relentless pursuit to undermine and ultimately eliminate what we value. The cultural war is, at its core, a spiritual battle.

Once we realize the spiritual nature of this fight, we see global events and the struggles of people around United States through a different vantage point. What is going on today is a direct manifestation of the Kingdom of Darkness' agenda to increase chaos and death on this planet.

The only Power that brings hope for true and lasting change in us and consequently in the world is the Lord Jesus Christ.

We have to reemphasize the resurrection life-power of Christ in the believer: "The Spirit of God, who raised Jesus from the dead, lives in you. And just as God raised Christ Jesus from the dead, he will give life to your mortal bodies by this same Spirit living within you."[1]

If we really comprehend how powerful His power within us is, we could, just like the early church, be accused of turning "the world upside down…"[2]

We need to rededicate ourselves to the One Who calls us to be: "a chosen people, a royal priesthood, a holy nation, God's special possession, that you may declare the praises of Him who called you out of darkness into His wonderful light."[3]

The demons in this story, like the current culture, mock Jesus and those who follow Him. Our duty is not to retaliate nor capitulate. We are to stand with the Sword of His Word. We are to be in full armor and fully prepared to engage the culture.

We are soldiers of the Cross, but what does that Cross represent? The Cross at its very core, shows us an undying, never-failing Love and His name is Jesus.

Jesus shows us a love that speaks the truth.

Jesus shows us a love that is willing to die.

Jesus declares to us a love that stands, unwilling to compromise but ever eager to pray for enemies, for many know not what they do.

Jesus is the very love of God Himself, "because God is love."[4]

We must not ever forget, however, a fundamental truth: We have read the end of the book, and we win. But until that Day, we fight with love, grace and a firm conviction that Jesus is Savior and Lord. Our only hope comes from repentance and a deeper walk with Jesus: "[I]f my people, who are called by my name, will humble themselves and pray and seek my face and turn from their wicked ways, then I will hear from heaven, and I will forgive their sin and will heal their land."[5]

So, we begin this modern story with a memorandum, sent from Heaven and written by an angel on a holy mission.

What this angel was able to obtain in the way of emails and documents confirms the High Court of Heaven's worst suspicions: the Dark Kingdom is on the move with an ever-increasing fury. We are allowed a peek into the inner workings of the Dark Kingdom, its agenda and methods through an exchange of emails between two demons.

Where do the United States and the Christian church appear in all of this? Right in the crosshairs.

All of these emails and documents are yes, satirical and hypothetical, but they do contain a deep warning.

It is a warning we should all heed.

Memorandum

From: The High Court of Heaven
To: Those Who Follow The Son
Subject: The Dark Kingdom is accelerating

    The Kingdom of our Almighty King ordered the NSA[1] to increase its surveillance of Planet Earth, due to a recent surge of the Dark Kingdom's activity across the globe.
    I, as an angel in the service of our glorious King, went undercover. I sought to gather intelligence to enhance the understanding of this activity. What you hold in your hands are the results of my covert operations.
    These communications confirm the High Court of Heaven's suspicions. The Dark Kingdom is on the move, with an ever-escalating influence over the United States of America and the Christian church in that country. We have learned that the Dark Kingdom will increase its assault on churches and families with an even greater vengeance and more blatant tactics.
    These emails and documents are very significant. They show the planning and guidance being done by one of the Dark Kingdom's leaders, Baal-Kobalt. This high-ranking demon's dominion is the United States of America. Baal-Kobalt has selected a low ranking demon named Wormwood.
    This Wormwood has been under our watch for a long time.

---

[1] Never Slumbering Angels [editor's note]

He first came to our attention when he was being tutored by his Uncle Screwtape, who sent him many letters on how to torment human beings. One of our very own servants, Mr. C. S. Lewis, brought these letters to light many years ago. They were published in 1942, in the midst of World War II. The Dark Kingdom was in a fury of activity during that dreadful time. We appreciated Mr. Lewis' efforts to inform a large number of people about demonic activity in his book, *The Screwtape Letters*.

Those letters were meant to mentor the young Wormwood, a then up and coming demon. His Uncle Screwtape guided him as he tormented a young man. Wormwood was not able, however, to prevent this young man from becoming a Christian. Wormwood's "failure" (not to us of course) resulted in him being sentenced to be consumed by his fellow demons.

Wormwood was apparently given a second chance. He has now been recruited for more intensive training by a new mentor, Baal-Kobalt. Wormwood was recently promoted by the Center of Hell under the recommendation of Baal-Kobalt. We now have incontrovertible evidence that Wormwood is a key figure in advancing the Dark Kingdom's agenda of reducing the United States to what these demons call "an irreverent and irrelevant nation."

Wormwood's targets, after his training, will be the Christian church and family in the United States.

We acknowledge that a large percentage of the U.S. population will find this information fanciful or improbable. One of the Dark Kingdom's most successful tactics is to convince people that it does not exist and that all history is guided by human beings alone.

For others, especially those who have confessed the Kingship of the Son, this information will be a confirmation of our glorious King's words, "I have told you these things, so that in Me you may have peace. In this world you will have trouble. But take heart! I have overcome the world."[6]

Many followers of our glorious King will be aghast at how much Scripture these demons use. Please remember that "You believe that God is one. You do well; the demons also believe, and shudder."[7]

These demons, in following the prince of this world, have learned the power of using the Blessed Word to their advantage. They may shudder from the knowledge, but they still know and use it, albeit in a corrupt way.

We wish for our glorious King's people to be more vigilant. We encourage His followers to eagerly put on the full armor of God and be ready to stand. The Son of our glorious King won, by His death on the cross and by His majestic resurrection, the very ground of hope and grace upon which His followers now stand. It is imperative that the King's sons and daughters now stand fast, holding the ground that He won for them against incursions by the members of the Dark Kingdom.

Those who love Him should be good soldiers, fighting with confidence the war that is already won, even if the outcome of individual battles seems uncertain. The Dark Kingdom only advances when those who are in the Kingdom of God do not heed the clarion call to defend the Gospel or stand steadfast when the battles intensify.

In these ever darkening days, our King's followers must walk in wisdom and in truth. They must walk in the Son and in Him alone. Jesus Christ is the very Wisdom of our Almighty Father. Human wisdom is not adequate for the days ahead. Only those in full amour and empowered by His Holy Spirit will be able to do exploits in our glorious King's name, Who is evermore to be praised!

Servant of the Most High,

Daniel

Chief Angel to the Western World
North America Operations
Dominion: United States of America

One final note: I have left the emails as they were originally sent, with their utterly disrepectful grammar, vocabulary and capitalization. It is a visual reminder of just how much hatred these demons have for all things holy.

NSA Release No. 1

Contents:
- Emails Establishing Contact Between Baal-Kobalt and Wormwood
- Wormwood's Promotion Letter
- Emails Reviewing Malevel 6.6.6

From: Wormwood <burnbabyburn@gothell.com>

To: Baal-Kobalt <capturetheplanet@brimstone.com>

Subject: Haven't heard from Uncle Screwtape in a while

Most Reviled Baal-Kobalt: The Center of Hell said that you would be my best contact to finding Uncle Screwtape. After having messed up with that christian back in the day, I was sentenced to be an appetizer in Hell. Wow, the thought of being gobbled up by my fellow demons was no picnic, let me tell you.

My uncle was so angry with me because I let that one human slip into the enemy's Kingdom. Yeah, I blew it, but hey, I was young and didn't know just how much power the enemy has over the hearts of his stupid children. I was given a second chance. I bet my uncle pulled some strings. Since then, I've worked harder! I've done as much evil as I could and I've rocked it!

I haven't heard from my uncle for a long time. I thought I should get a hold of him and let him know that yes, I learned something from him! Wormwood

From: Baal-Kobalt <capturetheplanet@brimstone.com>

To: Wormwood <burnbabyburn@gothell.com>

Subject: Your Uncle Screwtape's promotion

It's so diabolically delightful to hear from you. Let me bring you up to date. We promoted your Uncle Screwtape to Africa. He is in charge of civil wars there and he has exceeded our expectations.

Our Dark Lord loves famine, murder and mayhem. The reason? Humans will raise their fists at the enemy and blame him for all the mess. We enjoy assassinating the enemy's character as often as we can by the chaos we create. Civil wars are a delightful way to stir up anger at the enemy.

So, in our Dark Lord's wisdom, we promoted your Uncle Screwtape to such an operation. He now evilly pursues his assignment.

We are well aware of your record. We are so glad that you contacted us. We have grand things in store for you.

> From: Wormwood <burnbabyburn@gothell.com>
> To: Baal-Kobalt <capturetheplanet@brimstone.com>
> Subject: I'm chill

I cannot lie: I love what I do. I got sick of my uncle constantly harping on me about my failure to do this or that. These past decades have been nice. I just do my thing: pester humans, tempt them, make sure the enemy's son is mocked and make faith look stupid. Sweet. Demondom doesn't get much better than that, huh?

> From: Baal-Kobalt <capturetheplanet@brimstone.com>
> To: Wormwood <burnbabyburn@gothell.com>
> Subject: Oh, yes, it CAN be better!

Demondom does get better than that, my uninformed imp. In your effort to redeem yourself, you now have accumulated enough Malice Points to be promoted to the highest Malevel. Leave the pestering of humans to less insightful demons.

You have a grand future ahead of you. We are eager to begin your training.

If you, however, do not take this offer, then perhaps being changed into a bubbling mud pot on the side of a volcano would suit you? You could boil and spit all day. Sounds delightful, yes?

From: Wormwood <burnbabyburn@gothell.com>

To: Baal-Kobalt <capturetheplanet@brimstone.com>

Subject: I'm in!

Let's do this! I guess those long decades of pestering paid off, huh? But, I am not sure what you mean by the highest Malevel. Fill me in.

To: Wormwood <burnbabyburn@gothell.com>

From: Baal-Kobalt <capturetheplanet@brimstone.com>

Subject: Your promotion letter

I am glad you are on board. You will need to have the larger picture. First of all, I am attaching your promotion letter. **This information is for your eyes only.** The last demon (was it Toxen or Scabooze?) who chatted about this information to some friends ended up as a grub, always being eaten, regurgitated and passing through some robin's intestine. His friends? They ended up as ants who loved excreted grubs.

> **Promotion to the Highest Malevel Hereby Granted to:**
> **Demon Wormwood**
> **Filed with the Center of Hell**
> **Approval Granted Upon Completion of**
> **Malevels 6.6.6 Review and Tactics Training**
>
> Our Most Unrighteous Demon Wormwood,
>   I, on behalf of the Center of Hell, congratulate you! We

applaud your efforts of taking down one human being at a time. The one-to-one ratio of demon to human is certainly effective and enhances the numbers entering our Dark Lord's Kingdom. Afflicting a human is a worthy enterprise for a demon of any skill level. Finding a human's weak spot and tormenting that person constantly is a fine calling.

But you, our malevolent Wormwood, need to move up in the work of our Dark Lord. A command has come down from The Center of Hell to accelerate the breakdown of the Western World with a special emphasis on the United States of America.

I, Baal-Kobalt, am the Lord over the Dominion of the U.S. I now have special instructions to accelerate its decline. Our Dark Lord, in His wisdom, has commented many times "So goes the U.S., so goes the rest of the world." Let me explain how you came to the Center's attention.

We have watched your performance under **Malevel 6: Target the Individual.** Under this Malevel, a demon can use subtle means to torment a person, such as a job loss, a persistent sickness, or a rocky relationship. A demon can also use forceful means, such as the loss of a child, a divorce, or some other catastrophic event. Either way, if that person walks away from the enemy, Malice Points are accrued and tallied to that demon's record.

You have caused, despite your earlier failure, many to enter the afterlife with denial of the enemy on their lips. Consequently, you have received enough Malice Points to move up.

Normally, we promote a deserving demon to **Malevel 6.6: Promote Group Identity.** This Malevel is focused on stirring up humans in groups, not just as individuals. We expect the demon here to promote and sustain ethnic tensions, race riots, genocides, civil wars—oh, the wonderful list goes on and on. We adore humans pitted against one another, in group against group, where civil unrest, mayhem, and death reign.

With enough points accrued at this Malevel, a demon is promoted to the one that is the nearest and dearest to our Dark Lord's heart: the destruction of a whole nation.

But, because of your Uncle Screwtape's status at the Center and your tenacity to carry on (despite early failures), we are going to allow you to skip the Group Malevel and serve under my department. You are now to enter the Malevel that focuses on bringing down a nation. Your domain, under my supervision, will be the United States of America. Your targets will be the christian church and the family.

In order for you to know the full program, you must be acquainted with **Malevel 6.6.6: Destroy The Nation.**

All three Malevels tap into the sheep-like nature of these disgusting humans. They always want to see themselves as improving, moving away from ideas that seem so antiquated to their modern, forward-thinking brains. We encourage this thinking, especially if "antiquated" equals "biblical." Humans long to be seen as enlightened. They rally under the banners of "modern," "tolerant," and the ever-so-self-righteous one of "progressive."

This rejection of the enemy's morality and these humans' subsequent grasping for a new morality is combustible material for just the right kind of demon to ignite. We see you as just that kind of demon. We just love to watch all hell break loose.

We will be sending you Malevels 6.6.6 for your review. We expect your full engagement with the material. We will then forcus on Tactics Training to fine-tune your skills and get you ready for more intensive warfare.

With Malignant Malevolence,

Baal-Kobalt

Lord of the Western World
North American Operations
Dominion: United States of America

> To: Baal-Kobalt <capturetheplanet@brimstone.com>
> From: Wormwood <burnbabyburn@gothell.com>
> Subject: Wow!

Awesome! When you see Uncle Screwtape, tell him thanks. Who'd thought that Hell could be so forgiving!?!

> From: Baal-Kobalt <capturetheplanet@brimstone.com>
> To: Wormwood <burnbabyburn@gothell.com>
> Subject: Starting with Malevel 6

Forgiving? No. Increasingly needed personnel? Yes. The Dark Kingdom is gearing up and we need all hands on deck. Or perhaps, to put it more clearly, we need all flames ablaze on deck.

I will be covering all aspects of Malevel 6.6.6 for your training.

In brief, **Malevel 6 targets the individual.** We forcefully encourage people to become enslaved to the self.

Malevel 6.6 focuses on group identity. We want individuals to identify as a group, and bow down to that group's values. We encourage groups to have values that are hostile to the enemy.

Malevel 6.6.6 focuses on destroying a nation. We do so by attacking the christian church and the family.

I will cut and paste sections from the Malevels 6.6.6 Manual and send them to you as emails. We will review them together. I will first go over Malevel 6, step by step, with my expert commentary. I expect you to comment. Your comments will be evaluated. No passive learning on my watch.

Our target is to bring as many humans as we can into the Dark Kingdom. While those who do not follow the enemy's son are also desirable, we take a special pleasure in undermining and destroying those who follow the son. Time is running short. Word has it that the enemy's son may soon be making his move.

Let us begin.

> Malevel 6 Objective: "To encourage the targeted individual to become a captive to the self, alienated away from the enemy."
>
> Step 1: By using popular culture, a shattered home, a weak church or a trauma to create spiritual uncertainty, the targeted individual will grow less confident in the claims that christianity makes.

Our Dark Lord has been accused of being the "Father of Lies." He, of course, takes that as a compliment. As long as confusion reigns—initiated by some sort of trauma, uncertainty, or hypocrisy—such perplexing doubts undermine the confidence people have in what they have been taught, especially if they were raised in church.

We strive to make people doubt the truth of what they know. If people question the truth they have been taught, then we can slowly poison the idea of "truth" itself. We whisper, *How do you know what is true? Can anyone ever really know the truth?* If truth cannot be known, then whatever people think is right and wrong is acceptable.

We are creating an atmosphere where we encourage people to doubt **everything**. We undermine any certainty they have.

Thus, the enemy's book and morality is called into question. People then begin to lose direction.

Even if people don't follow the enemy's son, they want some kind of morality. We encourage them to create their own right and wrong, as far removed from that detestable book as possible.

We are creating, above all else, **confusion.** The Dark Lord has been accused of being the "author of confusion." He takes that as a compliment as well.

If we can get people to doubt everything they know, especially faith in the enemy, that, (despite what the enemy's awful book says) is the beginning of wisdom: **our kind of wisdom.**

> From: Wormwood <burnbabyburn@gothell.com>
>
> To: Baal-Kobalt <capturetheplanet@brimstone.com>
>
> Subject: Lies

Hey BK! If you throw in enough doubt about everything, then people think everything could be a lie. Doubt and lies are awesome at gutting what people believe, especially when what that book teaches doesn't match what people really do.

Go on about loving one another "until death do us part," then WHAM! Get a divorce!

Go on about the enemy's son being so loving and forgiving, then WHAM! Do horrible things in the son's name!

Go on about forgiving your enemy and then WHAM! Drop bombs on them in the name of freedom!

Blah, blah, blah about truth, justice and being a christian nation and then WHAM! Have the government do bad things to its citizens because all it really wants is power and control!

Yup, I could go on and on. Hammer truth with loads of lies and soon "truth" itself is a lie.

The word BELIEVE itself has the word LIE smack-dab in the middle of it. So true.

From: Baal-Kobalt <capturetheplanet@brimstone.com>

To: Wormwood <burnbabyburn@gothell.com>

Subject: We picked you for a reason!

Your enthusiasm is noted. Let us proceed on reviewing Malevel 6, shall we?

> Step 2: Alienate this person from the moral foundation founded on the enemy's principles.

Repeatedly remind people that throughout history, those who have followed the enemy and his principles have done so miserably. Show them the abundant hypocrisy in those who follow the enemy today. Church leaders, teachers and parents who have fallen into disrepute are particularly instructive for our purposes.

Repeat the idea over and over that the enemy's principles are utterly incompatible with a modern, tolerant and enlightened society. Make his principles look backward and distasteful. Guide people to principles that other human beings have created. Even better: Encourage people to create their own. Keep insinuating how limited, unenlightened and destructive the enemy's principles really are.

Whisper endlessly that true freedom comes only when **you** are in control. "Who better than you?" is especially potent, for now a person's pride is ignited. It is very easy to manipulate the sinful nature that a person possesses. Tapping into a person's pride is especially effective for manipulation and control by us.

Next, compound the ever-growing emptiness inside people's hearts. The enemy created these maggots for fellowship with Him. These maggots need something to worship; it is part of who they are. Without the enemy in their hearts, humans become lost, and will start grasping for something or someone else to love. What they love, they end up worshipping. A life without the enemy leads to being lost.

How our Dark Lord loves the lost.

Now, propose two options to these confused and empty people. Help them find their way, which is really the Dark Kingdom's way.

First, you can present a new object for people to worship, one that will give their life meaning. Culture, political activism, some new philosophy, a person, a lifestyle or a group will all do nicely. In other words, focus your captives' attention on some kind of idol: someone or something to love instead of the enemy. Our Dark Lord loves it when the maggots choose an idol, because there is always a new one available, just as the old one falls down or the person loses interest. We must keep a parade of new ones marching into people's lives.

The second option is to whisper that life is ultimately meaningless. As people question why they are here and what their purpose is, whisper that they are just an accident of evolution. Insinuate that they are only a collection of molecules…drifting, merely existing, and the only sure thing is a date with the dirt someday.

Whisper:

- *There is no heaven or hell! They're just meaningless myths.*
- *You are an unimportant creature, an accident, a product of random forces.*
- *You are nothing but worm food. Dirt you are and dirt will be your end.*
- *You have no purpose and no meaning.*

Our Dark Lord especially loves it when these maggots buy into the meaningless option.

We highly recommend that you encourage your captives drowning in "my life has no meaning and neither do I" to go out and hurt themselves and/or hurt others. The suicide of the young brings such pleasure to the Dark Lord, especially if this person takes others with them in a murderous rampage.

The enemy built these maggots to find fulfillment in only Him. We must do everything we can, my demon, to derail the enemy's design.

From: Wormwood <burnbabyburn@gothell.com>
To: Baal-Kobalt <capturetheplanet@brimstone.com>
Subject: Humans are just idiots

Hey BK! Humans lovin' themselves and not the enemy goes back a long way, huh?

I remember learning in Evil Academy how our Dark Lord went into the enemy's garden as a snake. Fantastic. He blended in so well in the branches of that forbidden tree that dumb-bunny Eve didn't even notice him. What was she doing hanging around that tree anyway? She had the whole garden and there she goes, wandering over to the tree where our Dark Lord was waiting. I love how he talked to her gently. He's a sly One! Even that book (may it burn) says that the Serpent was "crafty."

I am glad our Dark Lord didn't show up as a rabbit or some other cutesy animal. Eve would have been so busy cooing over it that she wouldn't have listened.

Eve was curious to see what this Snake was saying. He showed up in the way I'd expect: sparking a human's curiosity. He kicks it wide open when He says, "Did God really say…?" Brilliant.

Our crafty Dark Lord was really saying to her and everyone to come:

- *Who ya gonna listen to? You or God?*
- *Who's in charge? You or God?*
- *You know best. Serve yourself.*
- *God will understand and support you. Just be you.*
- *If you tick God off, he'll forgive you. He's all about love, love, love.*
- *Hey, it's also true he's a Cosmic Kill-Joy. Just go live it up.*
- *You know what's best for you. Take control.*

Eve and Adam went their own way. Our Dark Lord saw to that. They blew off the enemy's warnings and jumped right in. Humans are still doing it. Humans just love falling on the ground before Self. That idol stands on Pride!

They love the self because we keep telling them that *Hey, **You** are all you need!* Get that pride goin' and you win every time.

> From: Baal-Kobalt <capturetheplanet@brimstone.com>
> To: Wormwood <burnbabyburn@gothell.com>
> Subject: On to Malevel 6.6

Well said! We know how the enemy hates idols. The old carved ones have gone out of fashion. But anything that a person loves becomes important. The more important it becomes, the greater its influence over the person's life. Enough importance will ignite a person's pride to start relying on this idol. Soon, this idol will crowd out the enemy from view.

The easiest idol of all to love is the self. Once a person is taken captive by the self and all of its desires, just wait and watch with amusement. The Dark Kingdom thanks you, Adam and Eve, for passing on your sin-filled souls to all of your children!

Now, let's go on to review Malevel 6.6. I eagerly await your comments.

> From: Wormwood <burnbabyburn@gothell.com>
> To: Baal-Kobalt <capturetheplanet@brimstone.com>
> Subject: Adam and Eve

Hey BK! Quick comment. I remember Baal-Sulphur at the Evil Academy teaching us that because our Dark Lord couldn't attack the enemy himself, He went after the next best thing: the enemy's children.

Adam and Eve royally blew it by ignoring the enemy's words and taking a big bite outta that fruit. Our Dark Lord then shot lots of chaos and confusion into creation. Death, disease, destruction...Creation ain't so "good," is it? That first chapter of Genesis is hilarious now.

After the Fall, the enemy's children were even kicked out of that Garden by the enemy himself! He said something about living forever in sin, if Adam and Eve had taken a bite out of that Tree of Life fruit. Sounds tasty to me.

These humans have been such easy targets ever since. It ain't just shootin' fish in a barrel. It's huntin' bear in a bathtub.

> From: Baal-Kobalt <capturetheplanet@brimstone.com>
> To: Wormwood <burnbabyburn@gothell.com>
> Subject: Moving on...

So true. It is just too easy to deceive and manipulate these humans. Their sin nature, handed down by Adam and Eve, is all we need. "The Fall" is aptly named: These stupid humans fall every time we scratch the itch of their nature. Let's move on to Malevel 6.6, shall we?

> The Objective of Malevel 6.6 is: "Encourage individuals to become captive to the identity of a group, one that is hostile to the enemy's values."
>
> Step 1: Prey on a fundamental need that humans have: the need to belong.

We exploit these humans' need to belong as they seek a group to identify with and join. Humans love to belong to something greater than themselves. A group fulfills that need. Eventually, an individual's identity merges into a group's identity. The reason is simple: humans hate to be alone. These creatures **need** each other.

The enemy knew this when he made Eve. He knew that Adam would be more fulfilled with someone by his side. The Dark Lord fixed that in a hurry. He deceived Eve and she deceived Adam. Pathetic, isn't it? Just get one of these stupid humans to cave in to the Dark Kingdom's agenda and they happily lead others down the same path. This need to belong serves us all too well.

That wretched book says, "There is a way that appears to be right, but in the end it leads to death."[8]

I am so glad that these stupid creatures don't **really** read that book.

Humans are not solitary beings. Present a group to them with some kind of purpose and history and they join. The groups we support must be hostile to the enemy and his values. Any group that appeals to human nature with an emphasis on pride is especially alluring to these maggots.

The reason is simple: Any time human nature can build a world without the enemy, with humanity in control, people will line up. In fact, the Dark Kingdom was quite proud when all those ancient people gathered to build the Tower of Babel, with pride as its foundation. We regretted how the enemy put an end to that by scattering everyone.

Give these stupid humans enough material to create an identity from and soon that identity becomes everything. Identity holds the group together. Identity becomes, in effect, a whole new world for people to inhabit. It's the modern Tower of Babel, with the same foundation: pride. Who needs the enemy then?

> From: Wormwood <burnbabyburn@gothell.com>
> To: Baal-Kobalt <capturetheplanet@brimstone.com>
> Subject: Kinda ironic

Hey BK! Ask anyone and they'll tell you, "I am my own person! I think and act for myself!" Just wait, and soon that same person is stampeding into a herd of like-minded cows mooing on about how "I think for myself!" Yeah, right.

> To: Wormwood <burnbabyburn@gothell.com>
> From: Baal-Kobalt <capturetheplanet@brimstone.com>
> Subject: Go figure

Well said. Really, the only good human is a dead one, burning eternally. Let us move on.

> Step 2: Having identified with a group, humans will align more and more with it and its values. They will hate having their group's identity questioned, because now they feel personally offended.

We fan the flames of grievances, past and present. History serves us well here. These humans remember all too well the wrongs incurred at the hands of others. No one really ever gets along for any period of time, and soon the grievances—real and imagined—pile up. Exploit history and make it a spur to think hatefully of other groups.

> Step 3: Make the group feel special by persecution.

Conflict seems to solidify group membership. Persecution means that the members must be onto something good, or why else would others try to stop them? Consolidate their identity in the group with opposition. Humans will whine and complain about being persecuted, but it gives them a sense of being special.

> To: Baal-Kobalt <capturetheplanet@brimstone.com>
>
> From: Wormwood <burnbabyburn@gothell.com>
>
> Subject: History that whines

Hey BK! I love watching humans feel soooo sorry for their ridiculous selves as they boo-hoo over their poor group's history. I especially love it when that history is made up or overblown. It's fun to hear them gripe about how they've been soooo wronged by others in the past. They use history to pick a fight with folks living today.

It's awesome when they target those who they think are getting in their way. Humans are soooo hypocritical. How dare they call the Dark Lord the "Father of Lies." Really? Humans are happy to create their own lies so they can wallow in self-pity. After a lot of wallowing, they go nuts, hurting anyone in their path.

The cry of "You've got this coming for all you've done!" is my kind of rock and roll.

> To: Wormwood <burnbabyburn@gothell.com>
>
> From: Baal-Kobalt <capturetheplanet@brimstone.com>
>
> Subject: So true, so true

Well observed. Humans are so easily deceived every time an intriguing idea comes blowing their way and tickles their ears. They form groups around the ideas, whether true or not. Groups are such effective weapons in the Dark Kingdom's arsenal.

But, that is the point, is it not? Let us continue.

> Step 4: Now the cycle of retribution begins. Persecution of the group makes it want to retaliate. Encourage the group to reject the enemy's value system that the punishment should fit the crime, and goad them into believing they must go after their enemies without mercy.

We, in our Dark Lord's service, love to incite these gullible humans to repudiate that "eye for an eye" idea. No! Make it a life for an eye, a torture session for a disrespectful word, a mass slaughter for a grievance and a genocide for a belief.

The enemy's son even advocated "praying for enemies…" Oh, please. Humans must perceive their enemies as creatures worthy only of ruthless handling or even death. Whatever moral high ground one group might possess at first must degenerate into recrimination and bloodshed on everyone's part. Thus, martyrs are made and the cycle continues.

Revenge is sweet, for it serves our Dark Lord.

Civil rights, legal restraints, constitutions and law enforcement are suspended to make right all the wrongs done to the group, whether past or present. It can be subtle or blatant, but in the effort to make things rights, restraint is lost. The identity of the group's members is then sealed in blood. Now, more history is being made.

The beauty of this is? We can step out any time and just let those human maggots do the dirty work for us. Their beliefs provide the fuel and each conflict is the tinder for the next conflagration. The art is learning when to drop in the match.

> To: Baal-Kobalt <capturetheplanet@brimstone.com>
> From: Wormwood <burnbabyburn@gothell.com>
> Subject: Cain and Abel

Hey BK! I love it when humans make their enemies into anything but human! Like bratty children, these humans will yell,

- *My group is not your group!*
- *My group is better than your group!*
- *My group should conquer your group!*
- *My group needs to get rid of your group!*

Awesome. Murder is always on the menu. I dig that the first act out of Garden of Eden was murder. Cain's anger made it easy to pester him about slamming Abel with a rock. One of my instructors, Baal-Verboten, shared with us his whisperings into Cain's ear:

- *Forget he's your brother!*
- *He doesn't deserve to live for making you look bad with his sacrifice!*
- *What's wrong with your fruits and vegetables? They're good enough!*
- *Who does Abel think he is, bringing that lamb? Why should he be favored over you?*
- *Is he special because he's being obedient? Get real. He's just kissing up.*
- *It doesn't matter what you bring…just bring something.*
- *He's always making you look bad!*
- *Are you just gonna sit around and let him get away with it? Again?*

Cain was such a sucker! Just get a group of Cains and set them loose on a group of Abels and BOOM! The blood will flow! I just can't believe how flippin' easy it is.

> To: Wormwood <burnbabyburn@gothell.com>
> From: Baal-Kobalt <capturetheplanet@brimstone.com>
> Subject: Let's keep going!

Yes, Baal-Verboten was personally trained by the Dark Lord. We celebrated whole-heartedly as Cain crushed Abel's skull. The Dark Lord loves to see His face reflected in a pool of blood.

Let us carry on.

> Step 5: Once these humans start only thinking of themselves as members of a special group, they will look for a group to blame for their problems. Enhance this contentious outlook by emphasizing the "Oppressor Group" idea in the society. The Oppressor Group can be based on race, religion, wealth or status—the only criterion for its position is that it had power in the past and continues to wield power today. Promote the belief that all problems faced by other groups are only because of the Oppressor Group.

Because humans are so inclined to misuse power, there will be an abundance of examples of the Oppressor Group having used power unfairly or brutally with other groups. In other words, the Oppressor Group's history will provide ample opportunity for other groups to hold it in contempt.

We hereby declare that for our purposes the Oppressor Group is to be identified as christians in the United States. This is absolutely crucial and should drive the destruction of the U.S. and the christian church. Because the U.S. was founded on christian principles, the Oppressor Group in the U.S. is easily seen as christian by many groups today fighting for their rights. Christians must be targeted for retribution by other groups whose values are opposed to the enemy and his son.

The history of humans shows that the Oppressor Group dynamic works with all kinds of groups, in every country on this ridiculous planet. Genocide, race riots, civil wars, and religious terrorism all illustrate this important dynamic of how an "oppressed" group, pitted against the "oppressor" group, will lead to murder. The Dark Lord always sees to that. That is why human history is so saturated in blood.

This Group Malevel is already working beautifully in the U.S. with many groups going after christians and their values, seeking to redress the oppression from the past and present.

Those groups coming against christians and their values must be encouraged to escalate. Utter destruction of the U.S. and christianity is our endgame.

> Step 6: Any good the Oppressor Group (christians for our purposes) has done in the past or is doing now must be called into question. Encourage focusing only the Group's mistakes and hypocritical behavior. Over time, seek to eliminate altogether anything positive associated with the Oppressor Group (christianity).

The educational system for the young is very useful in facilitating this. Any good done by christians must be reduced to having suspicious motives. Insinuate that their real motives were (and still are) greed, control, abuse and debauchery. This will tarnish any good done by christians throughout history. History is full of christians speaking holy words but swayed by Hell's most debased imaginings.

By casting a despicable light on christianity's history, all we do is sit back and wait. Christians themselves will begin to shudder about how hypocritical christianity has been.

Christians will begin feel ashamed. They won't be able to evaluate their faith objectively any more. Because christians have been powerfully influential in U.S. history, we have a rich selection of mistakes and hypocritical behavior to continually emphasize:

- *Why were witches hung in Salem and not forgiven?*
- *Why was slavery allowed and how could christians even own slaves?*
- *Why were Native Americans treated so horribly?*
- *Why were Blacks subjected to segregation and lynching?*
- *Why didn't the U.S. help out the Jews during World War II?*
- *Why was the U.S. the first nation to drop the atomic bomb?*
- *Why were gays victimized with such oppressive laws?*
- *How can christians claim to be the only true faith in a pluralistic society?*

We want to undermine christians and everything they've done (whether true or not) in the U.S. This helps to create a list of endless grievances that demand action from those groups who see themselves as having been wronged.

Our goal is to make the christian heritage of the U.S. contemptible.

Ignorance of christianity's contributions to U.S. history and only focusing on its failures will undermine any positive associations christianity has as a moral force. Public schools and higher education are great assets here. They have been leading the vanguard for many years undermining and ignoring christianity's positive contributions to the U.S., such as abolition, the building of hospitals and orphanages, promoting equality and justice, and giving millions of dollars to charity (itself a christian value).

While many christians are not shrinking back in shame from their history and are facing the culture with a vigorous defense of the gospel, others have such shame about the past that they are not responding to the current changes we are pushing. The Dark Lord is pleased.

To: Baal-Kobalt <capturetheplanet@brimstone.com>

From: Wormwood <burnbabyburn@gothell.com>

Subject: Moo!

Hey BK! Humans have always found safety in numbers. Kinda like cows. Whether you call it a tribe, a clan, an ethnic group, a nationality or whatever, it's still a group. The individual gets lost in the group. Everybody moves with the herd. All ya gotta do is say the group's name and everyone else "knows" you. So, if you say you are a christian, people look at you and say, "No need to know any more. I know what your religion has done. You're one of *those* people." The christian soon shuts up, so he won't have to eat his lunch alone.

Stay quiet, pitiful believer. Your silence is golden as the Dark Kingdom presses on!

To: Wormwood <burnbabyburn@gothell.com>

From: Baal-Kobalt <capturetheplanet@brimstone.com>

Subject: Guilt…the gift that keeps on giving

Your comments are noted. Let us continue.

Step 7: Once the oppressed groups constantly remind christians of their history of hypocrisy, christians will step aside out of shame and guilt. Christians will want to appear enlightened. Their remorse will lead them to offer restitution, whether admitting to all the accusations or by keeping silent. Christians will desperately seek to break free from this blighted past.

Encourage other groups that have hidden in the shadows to now boldly walk into the light of day. Christians, not wanting to repeat history by offending them, will stay increasingly silent. Christians in the U.S. seem to be growing quieter all the time as other groups are clamoring for their rights. Bravo.

To: Baal-Kobalt <capturetheplanet@brimstone.com>

From: Wormwood <burnbabyburn@gothell.com>

Subject: Curse that book!

Hey BK! If ya hit christians, you gotta hit their book. For years, the church of the enemy's son has been way too influential in the U.S. Yuck. That blasted book has been, throughout its history, a mighty force against our attacks.

For every loser or hypocritical bunch that sported the enemy's name, there's been many others who stood on that book and what it says. They tried to build a better society based on that book.

The enemy's son psyched up his followers by saying even Hell's gates can't win against his church.

I remember our teacher Baal-Plagueit telling us that we must hunt down that book and kill it. He said, "Make the church squirm with those passages that are so out of step with modern thinking or that have been used to do terrible things in the past!"

The church today wants to see itself as progressive, tolerant, relevant. It wants to run as fast as it can away from its ugly past. The larger culture (ours!) is finally getting to the church. Right on.

Ah, what's a poor church to do? Huck out Biblical values.

Now you gotta a vacuum. Turn to the culture and snuggle up with its values. Invite the world to your pious dinner. Serve the world. Don't try to change it. Don't offend it. Do all of this in the name of love, love, love. Forget that part where the enemy's son talks about how love and truth go together. But truth costs ya. Nobody, including the enemy's followers, wants to be *that guy*. But if you lie down with the cultural dogs, you get fleas.

Doubts? Just look at what the culture has done to christian holidays. Take Christmas. The enemy's son coming to save the planet is lost to gift cards, shopping malls, traffic and spend, spend, spend. Easter? Even better! The enemy's son dying to save the planet is lost to chocolate bunnies, colored eggs and ham (of all foods!).

If the enemy's book is not front and center, what else will christians listen to but the culture? After a while, it get harder and harder to tell the difference between what the church believes and what the culture says.

The Dark Lord applauds as the cultural parade goes by, taking the enemy's kingdom right along with it.

Kick christianity to the cultural curb. Then get rid of it, like garbage.

Our instructor taught us about those times when the church did take a stand using that blasted book. As you said, many social causes, such as the abolition of slavery and anti-abortion laws, movements for social reform and racial equality, were fought in the son's name and that book.

Today, if the church does take a stand, we gotta push back. Hammer home that the church is full of ideas that have put down folks in the past, and still does! To those outside of the church, they will want to steer clear of such a backward bunch of idiots. To those inside the church, they'll cringe when the culture clashes with the book. Get those churchy types to look somewhere else for guidance. Get them to doubt the truth of those passages that are so hateful to modern thinking. Maybe they will start to doubt the whole book. Rock on.

It's especially cool when pastors stop preaching those verses that are outta step with the culture. Churchy types end up getting a cut-down version of that book. It's Bible-Lite, 80% less offensive than the whole enchilada. It's a man-made version—the kind we like.

That blasted book has the nerve to say it must be taken hook, line and s(t)inker: "All Scripture is inspired by God and is useful to teach us what is true and to make us realize what is wrong in our lives. It corrects us when we are wrong and teaches us to do what is right."[9]

The enemy's followers should cherry-pick only those verses that don't tick off the culture. The rest? Ignore 'em. Cherry-picking is awesome, 'cause it moves our agenda forward. Just pick those verses on love and acceptance.

C'mon, preachers: Make the enemy into a big, loving cosmic Buddy, who has a wonderful plan for your life and isn't looking to change you. He wants you to be a happier and more prosperous person! He wants you to live your "best life." (Not a life **of truth**, Hell forbid!) Shelve all that Hell-and-judgment-stuff! It just doesn't fit that big-Cosmic-Buddy thing. If you water down that book, you preachers are helping us!

Baal-Plagueit once told me, "Irrelevant book = Irrelevant church." Yup.

To: Wormwood <burnbabyburn@gothell.com>
From: Baal-Kobalt <capturetheplanet@brimstone.com>
Subject: You have been well taught!

Yes, slowly eliminating or perverting that book in the hearts and minds of the enemy's followers does make it easier to keep evil going on this repugnant planet.

We will soon get to the heart of the matter. Our goal is to make the U.S. irrelevant along with its christian heritage.

The Group Malevel has been applied increasingly to both the christian church in America, and as a bonus, to America itself. Many groups and other nations now see the U.S. as the cause of all the world's problems.

We are seeing the results of our efforts. The world hates America. The world persecutes christians. It's like the World Cup for the Dark Kingdom: Bring everyone together over their hatred of the U.S. and christians and let the games begin!

Let us continue our review of Malevel 6.6.

> Step 8: Unlike christianity itself, downplay any bad done by the groups that are now seeking recognition. Encourage the view that unacceptable behaviors only come from being oppressed. Once these groups are free, they will be everything christianity is not: tolerant, accepting and diverse.

Christianity needs to be seen as responsible for any regrettable behavior or actions taken by the oppressed groups as they fight for their rights. Minimalize personal responsibility in these oppressed groups. Promote only blame. Promote the idea that if christianity is removed from the U.S., all oppressed groups will finally be free. They will become all that they should be.

Acceptance and equality sound so reasonable.

But we know, from these maggots' history, acceptance and equality do not lead to harmony. Eventually (at our urging, of course!) the oppressed groups become so intoxicated with power that they will attack their former oppressors with a vengeance. Innocents die right along with the so-called guilty. The new leaders become worse than the ones they replaced.

This see-saw of history has provided the Dark Kingdom with endless hours of entertainment. The future for slaughter is always bright. In the end, what matters most to these "liberated" humans is having power and control and making others pay. Oppression doesn't ennoble humans—it makes them long for the day they are in power and can seek **revenge.**

Even those who follow the enemy's son can be seduced into thinking that they can handle power. Even well-intentioned people can fall prey to power's promise of control. How many prominent evangelists and pastors have acted as if they were in control only to fall from grace?

The enemy's son advocated the power of love. So boring. We advocate the power of control.

Look how the enemy's son tried to take over the world: by forgiving sin and empowering his followers to demonstrate his love by loving and caring for others.

At first, the early church seemed to live out the son's message of love and forgiveness for everyone. Even all that Roman persecution we threw at the early church could not put out that fire of the son's love in his followers.

Later, the followers of the enemy reached a point where they were no longer persecuted. Worldly temptations and the desire to rule became so seductive that the "Let's love them into the Kingdom" method grew boring. The church went from a group of followers to The Church and It became all powerful, all controlling.

We had ringside seats to such enjoyments as the Inquisition and the Crusades. It is so much more appealing to us when people are forced to convert. Burning at the stake, fear and torture are much more satisfying to His Darkness.

But I digress.

> Step 9: Soon, "evil" will have only one definition: the beliefs, behaviors and then the mere presence of christians in the U.S.

The presence of christians who truly follow the son and will not compromise is very irritating to His Darkness. We want others to join Him in His hatred of christians and create a willing army for us. "Evil" must be associated more and more with christianity.

Once "evil" becomes used against christianity **alone**, the word loses its connection with us.

Soon, some people will advocate, "We'd be better off as a society **without** christianity!" Bravo! Yes!

Real evil, our kind of evil, is then not so obvious. It's obscured under the rhetoric of politically-correct thinking.

When we finally release true evil, these useless humans will no longer recognize it. We are progressing nicely here and many groups are calling for christians to shut up and sit down.

Even some christians are calling for this as well. Many churches are obliging the call, all in the name of tolerance and love.

One fine day, people will call for christians to be silenced by any means necessary. Meanwhile, we keep our eye on the prize: We are preparing the way for our Dark Lord's Man of Action. If the U.S. is rendered useless along with the church, it can't stand up against our devices and our chosen World Leader.

That book calls him the "Antichrist." We like that name, because not only does "anti" mean "against," it also means "in place of." We want to replace the enemy's son and his followers. We are scheming to put our Son—our Man of Action--and His followers in power. The road to His glory is paved with the rhetoric of tolerance that seeks to right the wrongs of the past. How lovely in thought, how deadly in action.

Now, summarize what you've learned about the Individual and the Group Malevels. We must not waste time.

To: Baal-Kobalt <capturetheplanet@brimstone.com>

From: Wormwood <burnbabyburn@gothell.com>

Subject: Putting it all together!

Hey BK! Here goes!

- *Get people so confused, angry and alienated that they look for a new identity.*

- *Christianity gets the boot 'cause it's way too hypocritical.*
- *Lure people to groups that makes them feel special and hate the enemy.*
- *Fan the flames in the U.S. with oppressed groups feeling angry at christians because of the past.*
- *Christians will feel shame for all that's said about them. They will back-pedal and bend over backwards to kiss up to those oppressed groups.*
- *These groups will see themselves as victims. They will worship themselves. They will slap each other on the back about how progressive they are. They're out to change history (with our help!)*
- *Plaster "evil" on everything that christianity stands for and promotes. Blame that book for every evil in the world and in the U.S., past and present.*
- *Once christianity's values are kicked to the curb, the gap will be filled with new set of values—"progressive" and "enlightened"--our kind of values!*
- *Someday soon, the Dark Lord will take on the world with His Man of Action. He will create the ultimate "progressive and enlightened" group and these ridiculous humans will fall over each other trying to join up. This new group will be everything christianity isn't: progressive and understanding. This new group will also be everything all oppressed groups want: non-judgmental and loving.*
- *Tolerance and love will be the order of the day.*
- *Finally, the church of the enemy's son will get what it deserves: persecution and elimination.*
- *We will reign 'cause we will have a willing army.*

But isn't there a Mark in this post-christian America's future? That wretched book calls it the "Mark of the Beast." How stupid. It will be the Badge of Tolerance. But if ya don't get one, watch out! So simple, even a baby demon could do it. How'd I do?

> To: Wormwood <burnbabyburn@gothell.com>
> From: Baal-Kobalt <capturetheplanet@brimstone.com>
> Subject: Good job!

You now see the larger picture. Right now, some groups are unknowingly doing the work of the Dark Lord—denying His very existence and yet being open to His influence. Some are knowingly doing His work because they love the darkness more than the light.

The future does hold the Ultimate Identity Group. It will be empowered by our Dark Lord. It will be headed up by our Man of Action, whose name will be spoken in hushed, reverential terms. His voice and face will be carried everywhere by every technology available. The World Wide Web will take on a more sinister arachnid quality.

Woe to those who do not join, however. We have special delights set aside just for them. Ponder this: A person will proudly bear the Mark for the Man of Action's group because it will represent the vanguard of progressive thinking. Without the Mark, you are nobody. Then, no body.

I, in our Dark Lord's service, am recruiting you to lead a mighty army, one that will get the U.S. and the enemy's church pushed to the margins and then eliminated. His Darkness be praised!

> To: Baal-Kobalt <capturetheplanet@brimstone.com>
> From: Wormwood <burnbabyburn@gothell.com>
> Subject: I gonna miss doing damage!

Hey BK! I'll miss getting down and dirty with the Group Malevel. Yeah, I am honored to skip a grade, so to speak.

Humans, one on one, can be decent (I gag as I write this) but put them in a group, and all you hear is "Baa, baa." They let the group think for them. Soon, the group is what defines them. It also confines them, but we dig that.

But, if you think about it, this Group Malevel is just a counterfeit to what the enemy has been doing in history.

First, he picked the Jews and then called out to everybody to join his family through his son: "There is neither Jew nor Greek, there is neither bond nor free, there is neither male nor female: for ye are all one in Christ Jesus..."[10]

We want groups at each other's throats. The son brings people together, singing "Kumbaya" and acting like family. Yuck.

The enemy taught the Jews and then all of humanity that his presence and his word is all they need: "He did it to teach you that people do not live by bread alone; rather, we live by every word that comes from the mouth of the LORD."[11]

We've tried to burn that idea. The enemy and his word are **not** what people need or want.

The enemy told his people not to think our way: "He did all this so you would never say to yourself, 'I have achieved this wealth with my own strength and energy.' Remember the LORD your God. He is the one who gives you power to be successful, in order to fulfill the covenant he confirmed to your ancestors with an oath."[12]

Fast forward to the U.S. People who came here saw themselves as a new Israel—a new nation founded on faith, with that book as the foundation. They wanted to honor the enemy as they created the U.S. government. They saw the

U.S. as a "city on a hill." Even today, some of the enemy's followers still call this a "christian nation." Gag.

But, just like the Israelites did in their history, the U.S. has turned its back on the enemy. Yeah, some of that biblical heritage is still around, on monuments and on public buildings. I love what the Dark Lord says, "Better carved in stone than carved on the heart." Stones can be ignored. Stones can be removed.

Look at the 4th of July! Americans today celebrate the birthday of a country that the founders wouldn't even recognize. It just cracks me up.

I dig how the Dark Lord messed with the Jews. He is now messing with the U.S. about this whole "chosen by the enemy" thing. The Jews went after others gods and left the enemy high and dry during their long biblical history. The U.S. is now doing the same thing.

I see the *Chosen to Frozen* parade going something like this:

- *We were chosen by him sometime ago in our history.*
- *We don't know why we were chosen but we are grateful to him.*
- *We live obediently in our gratitude and are proud to be his.*
- *Our obedience yields blessings and his blessings multiply.*
- *We soon grow self-satisfied and lazy.*
- *We see his blessings more and more as coming from what we do, not from him.*
- *We rely on us more and more and we thank him less and less.*
- *We accomplished more and more and we call on him less and less.*

- *We find we really don't **need** him anymore. We can do it ourselves.*
- *Who is he? We are not so sure anymore. He becomes increasingly irrelevant.*
- *Soon, he and his values are thrown away.*
- *We now will need to update our values to show just how far we've come.*

The new values are delivered right to the nation's door, compliments of the Dark Kingdom! Malevel 6.6 is working in America, for sure. Many groups are now trying to erase the christian heritage of the U.S. Boo-yah! Seeing those stupid Ten Commandment monuments cast onto the scrapheap of history is so cool. It's about time the U.S. got a new history!

Christians do seem to be growing quieter. As the silence grows, the only voice we will hear is hatred! My kind of music.

> To: Wormwood <burnbabyburn@gothell.com>
> From: Baal-Kobalt <capturetheplanet@brimstone.com>
> Subject: That blasted book

The biggest obstacle for creating and sustaining identity groups is that blasted book—it is a burr under the progressive saddle. The enemy wants his creatures to have their identity only in him, based on the promises of his word.

That traitor Paul says: "For Christ himself has brought peace to us. He united Jews and Gentiles into one people when, in his own body on the cross, he broke down the wall of hostility that separated us...."[13]

Tearing down walls, indeed. Human-built identities create walls, and walls lead to anger and suspicion. The Dark Lord loves walls—the higher, the better. Divide and conquer is our Dark Lord's way. Our goal is simple: bloodshed and death. Our method is simple: Fight the son by destroying his followers.

> To: Baal-Kobalt <capturetheplanet@brimstone.com>
>
> From: Wormwood <burnbabyburn@gothell.com>
>
> Subject: Twist that blasted book!

Hey BK! I learned a lot in Evil Academy about how our Dark Lord faced off with the enemy's son back in the day. Our Dark Lord turned the enemy's own words around and used them against the son.

The son was hanging out in the desert after his baptism by that loser John. The Dark Lord showed up in His clever way: He always hits the enemy's children at their most vulnerable. And whoa, that son was hungry.

Our Dark Lord whispered into the enemy's son's ear: *How about turning stones into bread, Mr. Forty-Days-Without-Food? No one will tell! Your power can be used for anything, including satisfying your hunger! No one will ever know that you used your power for such a little thing. It's all good!*

Earlier, the son got the enemy's approval and power as he rose up out of the water. The Dark Lord was only trying to make some suggestions on how the son could use this new power: *How about stones to bread? No problem for you. Piece of cake.*

The Dark Lord then ramped up how to use that power: *Hey! You got the power now! OK, don't use it for personal stuff, but for an honorable cause: building up your ministry. How about jumping off the Temple in a spectacular display to gain followers? No worries and no injuries! People will line up after they see you do such wonders! Everyone loves a big show of power! You'll just walk down the street and everyone will follow you!*

The Dark Lord's Man of Action will use lots of miracles and big power displays to get people to follow him, for sure!

(I'd have told the son: *Want REAL success on this planet? Partner up with its Owner! If the Dark Lord once served in Heaven with your father, why not serve on this earth together? The Dark Lord and the son. What a combo!*)

The Dark Lord, as always, nailed it when He came after the son the third time: *How about gaining all the kingdoms of the earth? All you must do is worship Me! If you desire to rule the world, go directly to its Prince! I am He and I give and I take away! I've got the whole world in My hands and I don't mind sharing with you, son of my enemy.*

The son sure blew it. He could've gone big in his ministry. Popular dudes don't have a cross in their future. The world doesn't nail people it loves.

I follow my Leader: I want to twist the enemy's words and make that book look stupid. If people don't believe in anything, they fall for everything. Our Dark Lord has plenty of everything!

To: Wormwood <burnbabyburn@gothell.com>
From: Baal-Kobalt <capturetheplanet@brimstone.com>
Subject: You nailed it!

You have been well taught.

We will now review the Nation Malevel. You have been hand-picked to operate in this Malevel. Learn it to where it is first nature. Our time is short.

> The Objective of Malevel 6.6.6 is: "To encourage the destruction of an influential nation; a nation with a christian heritage is a top priority."
>
> Step 1: By deploying both the Individual Malevel and Group Malevel consistently, we can encourage the targeted nation to become self-focused, angry and narcissistic.
>
> Step 2: Give this nation a sense of defeat, disgusted by its past. Rewriting history to serve this end is critical. There is no shortage of those who despise their country and are willing to aid in its demise.
>
> Step 3: History then becomes an unescapable burden and the nation's energies are focused on redressing grievances or on distractions that feed the self. Get enough shame and blame going, and they become a potent mixture, leading to apathy.

We are increasing our focus on the U.S. per His Darkness' command. The U.S. has been influential in helping other nations because of its christian values. If christians are marginalized to a point of disappearing, then the U.S. loses its moral direction as well as its action. We kill two obnoxious birds with this Malevel's stone.

Comments, my deadly demon?

To: Baal-Kobalt <capturetheplanet@brimstone.com>

From: Wormwood <burnbabyburn@gothell.com>

Subject: If you're human, you've done evil

Hey BK! The enemy calls us evil? How 'bout those maggots he made? They burn people, build crematoria, dig mass graves and have lots of tortured bodies to throw in! Yeah, we cheered them on, but c'mon! We only whisper…humans act! Adam and Eve made sure that humans blow it, big time, 'cause it's their nature! Everyone's got something to regret, even if they think they're pretty good overall. That's why the enemy sent his son to be the savior—these maggots **so** need saving from themselves and from us.

That's why I love to bug people with all the bad stuff they've done, either now or back in the day. A nation is no different, and the U.S. has lots to feel guilty about. So, I get it. Pester people about what their country has done wrong in the past, and with their guilt in full swing, they'll want to get it right.

Mix sincere folks with prideful folks trying to fix the country without that blasted book's guidance and we win! They'll mess it up even more. Society will go down, down, down, and who will they blame? The very cosmic bad guy they say they don't believe in! It just cracks me up. Even if they don't know that book, people still blame the enemy, even if they have no clue about who he is. People who don't follow him or even believe in him still like to have him around to point a finger at when it all goes south.

I just hand them a shovel so they dig an even deeper hole to throw their faith and nation into! Our Dark Lord always has shovels on hand.

To: Wormwood <burnbabyburn@gothell.com>
From: Baal-Kobalt <capturetheplanet@brimstone.com>
Subject: Spot on!

Yes. To undermine faith and a nation, sometimes all you need is a word. A loaded word. Particularly effective today are these detonators:
- racism
- civil rights
- human rights
- sexism
- homophobia
- intolerance
- gender identity
- capitalism
- corporations
- christianity
- white privilege

Couple these with grievous examples from history and you can completely undermine a modern nation. We must be subtle but steadfast as we proceed.

If we are too blatant, there will be backlash. Some followers of the son as well as the more conservative members will push back. If we move too quickly, there will equally be backlash. Be subtle. But be relentless.

Remember: Humans just love to imagine themselves as being enlightened. Anything that feeds these humans' need to feel self-righteous (what that book calls "pride") we just keep pushing and encouraging.

Humans eagerly rewriting their history and seeking to be a more tolerant society provide such fertile ground for putting this Malevel into operation.

That book says that it was pride that caused our Dark Lord to be exiled from heaven. He countered with His motto: "Better to be a king in the darkness than a slave in the light." Pride for us is a good thing. We are able to exploit it so easily in human nature.

Humans are our target for one reason: The enemy never ceases to desire fellowship with his humans. He even calls himself "jealous..." He won't tolerate any idols. He wants his humans to love only him.

We attack the enemy through his creatures. As our Dark Lord reigns over this petty planet Earth, we have it made in the shade. We're a shark in the dark! (I am starting to sound like you, my pesky Wormwood! The Dark Lord help me.)

Let us proceed with the Nation Malevel's next step.

> Step 4: Blame christians and the United States for everything that has gone wrong and is going wrong, including acts that were once thought to have been done by enemies. Sow the seed of dark conspiracies that always lead back to the United States and its involvement. The ultimate conspiracy must be seen as christianity's influence over the United States.

I love this one because we can slip out of the chaos we create without even being noticed. Someone else gets the blame—never us. True, some christians will say this is spiritual warfare, being conducted by the Dark Kingdom against the enemy and themselves. But with them in the societal doghouse, as it were, who is listening?

Comments?

To: Baal-Kobalt <capturetheplanet@brimstone.com>
From: Wormwood <burnbabyburn@gothell.com>
Subject: I love them conspiracies!

Hey BK! I love how the September 11th terrorist attacks went from bad guys flying planes into buildings to the U.S. President setting it all up so his approval rating would go up! Awesome! It all started by sowing doubt in people's minds. Soon, with enough weird evidence flying around and a smear campaign going on about the U.S. and its intelligence gathering, people grew skeptical.

The Dark Kingdom turned that bit of history around! The U.S. was no longer a victim of a terrorist attack. Many people believe that the U.S. created and then used this event to invade and conquer the Middle East. Lots of folks in the Middle East especially bought this. The U.S. has since gained even more enemies!

People are now ashamed of the U.S.'s presence in the world. Boo-yah. Making this christian nation the biggest bad guy on the block is a 2 for 1! People now believe that if you pull back the curtain of the real evil in the world today, you'll find the U.S. They also say that the U.S. hides its real agenda; only those who "get it" understand the true goings-on. Keep those conspiracies coming! Because conspiracies supposedly have secret knowledge, those who "get it" always feel so self-righteous. They love lording this knowledge over others.

Bottom line: If all the bad stuff comes from some kind of conspiracy, then the average Joe can sit on his butt. If conspiracies are really running things, why bother to look further into why things are so messed up?

So, blame leads to shame. Those dumb humans clam up. Nothing gets done.

Shame leads to bending over backward to be seen as nice. Nothing gets done.

Feeling helpless against unseen forces means, yup, you guessed it: nothing gets done.

Nice. The goal of all of this? No one gives a rip. People get suckered into thinking that things happen not because of human choice but because of those conspiratorial puppeteers who pull the strings and make all the bad stuff happen. The good stuff gets done by all those progressive folks. Bad stuff? You guessed it! America and those bible-thumpers. Someday, under our Man of Action, christianity will be painted as The Conspiracy of All Conspiracies and will be deep-sixed. (Or is that deep six-six-six?)

I'm stoked. I get to sow doubt in the minds of young people about everything the U.S. and christianity stand for. I love to hound the young with questions like:

- *Is anyone really telling the truth?*
- *How can you really know?*
- *Is there even a truth?*

Results? Apathy torments young people today like ticks on a naked hiker.

Get this thinking into the enemy's followers and you get a crisis of faith! They may even split from the faith.

Apathy is cool. Spiritual apathy is way cool. Being apathetic keeps you spiritually lifeless. You don't call on the enemy 'cause you really don't know him. You live a zombie-life: walking, talking but not really living.

So, apathy is a win for our Kingdom. If you stay dead in your sins, and don't respond to the call from the son to leave your grave, or you follow him but stumble and fall all the time, the enemy's kingdom does not move forward.

If that book and those who follow the son are not around to be any threat to our work, then the day a human croaks, that guy is just dog-in-the-dirt dead. He ain't calling on the son then. *Too late, buddy. You're now hanging out at our eternal jukebox, sweatin' and regretin'.*

Some call it hell. I call it awesome.

> To: Wormwood <burnbabyburn@gothell.com>
> From: Baal-Kobalt <capturetheplanet@brimstone.com>
> Subject: Undermine, undermine, undermine

Yes! Faith in the enemy is so counter-productive to the Dark Kingdom. Faith leads to action. People who are truly alive in the son will respond to brokenness in others. These folks actually love others enough to help them. Disgusting.

That stupid brother of the enemy's son, James, said: "What good is it, my brothers and sisters, if someone claims to have faith but has no deeds? Can such faith save them? Suppose a brother or a sister is without clothes and daily food. If one of you says to them, 'Go in peace; keep warm and well fed,' but does nothing about their physical needs, what good is it? In the same way, faith by itself, if it is not accompanied by action, is dead."[14]

The less faith there is, the less the followers of the enemy get out in the world and work to make a difference for the enemy's kingdom. That means we can work our agenda more and more. Let us continue the review.

> Step 6: Anything negative, past or present, that can be exploited to cast an unfavorable light on christians and the United States must be emphasized in every way possible, so that national shame will turn into overcompensation. Shame will drive people to distance themselves from their country and its concerns. They will then seek to be as tolerant as possible, which will eventually lead to apathy.

Comments?

> To: Baal-Kobalt <capturetheplanet@brimstone.com>
> From: Wormwood <burnbabyburn@gothell.com>
> Subject: Baby, I was born that way!

Hey BK! The power of shame is the gift that keeps on giving. Just mention the word "slavery" and "racism" and the debate comes to a screeching halt. Compare being black to being gay and the door of shame swings wide open.

People don't want to repeat history by now being bigoted against gays, so they shut up quickly. People scramble to make new policies that dump biblical morality. They're trying to get it right this time. People hate appearing backward.

Those who follow the enemy are no different. They want respect from the culture for not repeating history. Making gay rights into civil rights is fantastic. This comparison is spot-on 'cause that book was used to support slavery and racism in all its ugly forms. Slaveholders, members of the KKK and society used that book to keep racial inequality alive and kickin'.

People now cringe at that. They run like scalded cats from any hint that they are like those bigots of not so long ago. Many believers distance themselves from others who use that book to speak out against gays, harping on that sin thing. Not wanting to repeat history when it comes to gays, the church is stepping back and joining the progressive parade. The "born that way" argument rings loud and clear.

That book says that humans are all "born that way." What "way"? Sinners in need of a savior. That loser Paul says, "For everyone has sinned; we all fall short of God's glorious standard."[15]

Kick that book to the curb. Water down its power by focusing on just a few verses here and there.

But, you gotta hear about the son to believe in him: "How then shall they call on him in whom they have not believed? And how shall they believe in him of whom they have not heard? And how shall they hear without a preacher? And how shall they preach, except they be sent?"[16]

But, you gotta preach all of that book to get the whole message. It's not just about gettin' saved—it's about becoming more and more like the son. Our job is to make sure that won't happen. Humans then won't have the enemy's power to make the sin nature weaker and his change in them stronger.

What's a human being to do? You're just born that way, man, and if ya can't beat it, join it. I'll cheer you on in the stands!

To: Wormwood <burnbabyburn@gothell.com>
From: Baal-Kobalt <capturetheplanet@brimstone.com>
Subject: Shocked and awed

I am surprised at you. Isn't tolerance the highest goal of this modern age?

To: Baal-Kobalt <capturetheplanet@brimstone.com>
From: Wormwood <burnbabyburn@gothell.com>
Subject: "Tolerance" makes me sick!

Hey BK! Tolerance. What a joke. It's just another word for people not giving a rip.

These maggots act so self-righteous about causes and issues, yet they won't give the time of day to some homeless guy holding up a sign. They'll sneer at his dirty clothes and drive away in their sparkly new Escalade. They refuse to make moral judgments, thinking that by tolerating some belief or action, they are more loving than those Bible-thumpin' folks who actually stand for something.

The truth is, if ya don't make a moral judgment, you can turn away and not worry about it. Tolerance is just another way these stupid humans shuck their responsibilities to each other. You can just hear how such people think:

- *If I see people standing on the Interstate and a semi-truck is bearing down on them, it is not my place to warn them. It's their choice.*
- *They were born to stand on the Interstate, freely expressing who they are. How can this be a problem? How can it be my problem?*
- *Oh, that book says it's a problem. Really? Well, that book counts for nothing. I think those people on the Interstate are brave as they follow their bliss.*
- *Be transgressive and face down the semi-truck of oppression! We should all celebrate such fearlessness!*

Bring on tolerance! It's a road block to biblical thinking and behaving! Road-kill on the Interstate of Indifference is such a blast.

To: Wormwood <burnbabyburn@gothell.com>

From: Baal-Kobalt <capturetheplanet@brimstone.com>

Subject: We are nearing completion

Your enthusiasm is condemnable!

We are on the home stretch, my willful demon. We have almost completed the review of the Malevel 6.6.6, where we bring down a nation with our agenda. When people grow tired and disgusted with what is going on around them, they withdraw into themselves. Because pride is so easily provoked in a person, such a withdrawal leads to a pre-occupation with the self. This is such rich soil for us to sow destruction in, and we do.

Here are the final steps:

> Step 7: Encourage narcissism in all social outlets, especially in the churches. Make pride (calling it "self-esteem") paramount. Drive home the message, "It's ALL about YOU."
>
> Step 8: With people engaged in such self-centered attitudes, the biblically-defined institutions of marriage and families will suffer. The ultimate goal: make these institutions appear so ridiculous that the culture will seek to redefine them—with our input, of course.
>
> Step 9: With the nation so preoccupied with its domestic front and its low view of itself, it will pull back from its leadership role in the world. It will become insular and unreliable. Other nations will come to distrust it. It will become a shadow of its former self, well on its way to be becoming useless.

Let me say this is the most satisfying of the Malevels. The destroying of a nation, especially one as powerful as the U.S., is a wonderful undertaking.

We will not just focus on stirring up group against group in the U.S. We are doing that already and it is producing wonderful results. The U.S. is extremely divided now. In fact, the last time it was this divided was just before the Civil War. That conflict lead to 600,000 people dying. The harvest of the dead is always satisfying. Yes, many went to the enemy with a prayer on their lips, but many died feeling alone and forsaken.

That's why division is so important: with sinful humans at the forefront, division usually leads to destruction and death. This is always the priority for the Dark Kingdom.

This is why we want to marginalize christianity and the U.S. We want to engage in a forceful spiritual war that will bring the whole disgusting U.S. edifice down, with its churches and christian heritage. Bring it all down into the flames of Hell.

The Dark Lord takes pleasure in knowing that the U.S. is slowly slouching towards destruction. You are part of this ignoble calling. Final thoughts?

To: Baal-Kobalt <capturetheplanet@brimstone.com>

From: Wormwood <burnbabyburn@gothell.com>

Subject: Not a summary but a quick formula!

Hey BK! While I respect the material that we've covered in the Malevels, I think we could simplify the whole shootin'-match. Here's "The Wormwood Formula": "Take this christian nation and make it **neither.**" So simple.

I am soooo ready to take on my assignment! Rock and roll!

To: Wormwood <burnbabyburn@gothell.com>

From: Baal-Kobalt <capturetheplanet@brimstone.com>

Subject: Final words—for now

Well done. One final point. The U.S. stands on three pillars:

- Its church with its teaching of judeo-christian values
- Its history with its foundation of judeo-christian values
- Its families and its modeling of judeo-christian values

Your assignment will be to continue shaking the ground that is sending cracks up those pillars every day. You will be responsible for weakening the family and the church in the U.S.

We have the universities and educational institutions in the U.S. assisting us with the rewriting of history. We support their claims that the U.S. contributes more than its fair share to the world's misery. We will continue to inspire such efforts.

You have done well in our review. I will certify you as ready to proceed to the Tactics Training for undermining the church in America and shredding the family as an influential unit. Once you have completed that, we will set you free to let all Hell break loose.

The Dark Lord welcomes you. We only see evil days ahead!

NSA Release No. 2

Contents:
- Emails Outlining Tactics Training between Baal-Kobalt and Wormwood
- Emails Detailing the First Target: The Christian Church in the United States

> To: Wormwood <burnbabyburn@gothell.com>
> From: Baal-Kobalt <capturetheplanet@brimstone.com>
> Subject: Let's begin

In order for you to operate at the Nation Malevel, you must first understand the tactics that the Dark Kingdom employs. We have reviewed the steps and you have done well.

We look forward to the day when you will go out fully prepared to assist in bringing the church and the U.S. to its knees, and I don't mean in prayer. Let's review: What is the goal of this Malevel?

> To: Baal-Kobalt <capturetheplanet@brimstone.com>
> From: Wormwood <burnbabyburn@gothell.com>
> Subject: No problem-o!

Here it is, Big Guy! "To encourage the destruction of an influential nation; a nation with a christian heritage is a top priority."

On a roll here: "So goes the U.S., so goes the world." Our Dark Lord's words of wisdom are so good. And so am I.

> To: Wormwood <burnbabyburn@gothell.com>
> From: Baal-Kobalt <capturetheplanet@brimstone.com>
> Subject: And you are modest as well!

Was it Moulde or Mildrewe that once got a bit too familiar with me and ended up a parasite in the gut of a Third World dictator?

I demand respect, my cheeky demon. Respect. Always keep that in your impish mind. You were rescued by me from being dined upon by your peers. I can always arrange an invitation to a dinner, with you at the head of the table. Youth will be served: On a platter, mouth stuffed with an apple. Agreed?

Let the Tactics Training begin. Our target is the church in the United States. Now, for a basic question: What is the purpose of the church?

> To: Baal-Kobalt <capturetheplanet@brimstone.com>
> From: Wormwood <burnbabyburn@gothell.com>
> Subject: church, schmurch

Hey BK! Sorry for the slip-up in the Respect Department.

If you were to ask that loser Paul, he'd say: "He is the one we proclaim, admonishing and teaching everyone with all wisdom, so that we may present everyone fully mature in Christ."[17]

Paul blathers on: "So Christ himself gave the apostles, the prophets, the evangelists, the pastors and teachers, to equip his people for works of service, so that the body of Christ may be built up until we all reach unity in the faith and in the knowledge of the Son of God and become mature, attaining to the whole measure of the fullness of Christ."[18]

Yeah. Yeah. Yeah. So, the church is the "body" of the enemy's son. This body is supposed to teach and build people up so they know the enemy's son better. If this body is working right, our wolves in sheep's clothing get noticed; people are so grounded in the son that they can spot that wolf costume a mile away.

Love is the blood that flows in this body. I say, attack it. People are wolf chow if they ain't reading that stupid book.

Let's dazzle them with "new" ideas. "New" ideas are the Dark Lord's old teachings repackaged for a new generation. Let's cause people to get all worked up over rules and regulations not found in that book.

Let's give "new" revelations so people will dash out and create a church that adds new stuff to that book. My favorite one to get that rolling is, "The son really isn't who he says he is." Like scalded chickens, out come all sorts of pride-bloated teachers with lotsa teachings, having "discovered" who the son really is! I dig the one about the son being the brother of Lucifer. Whoa. That one rocks.

The son should be at the church's center—he's the head after all. He makes the church powerful and alive. Let's make the church weak by putting down, recasting or booting out the son altogether. We'll then get our kind of church: powerless, man-made and one that makes folks feel special.

Why special? Because despite what that book says, they got something new to blather on about: a new spin, a new revelation, a new book, and a new way of doing stuff.

All the while we're laughing. They're walking off the pier into a sea of hungry sharks. "Work to make the church nothing but a chum-bucket" is how Baal-desTroy once put it. Yup.

To: Wormwood <burnbabyburn@gothell.com>

From: Baal-Kobalt <capturetheplanet@brimstone.com>

Subject: It's all about you!

Your ideas are well taken.

Let us now explore a strategy that churches have been employing for quite some time that we can exploit: churches want to grow. They want more and more sheep to hear the message. They want to fulfil the son's commission to evangelize this miserable planet. Then people feel good about their church. Some churches promote going out into the world to share about the enemy's son.

We prefer when churches are country clubs with that book stuck under their pews. No growth on the inside--I don't mean numbers, I mean the heart--means no growth on the outside. We delight in those churches that are morgues filled with The Frozen Chosen: no life, no growth.

Churches know that it is only under the enemy's leading that the church will grow. But far too often the enemy takes way too long for human tastes. So, to fulfill the son's commission, many churches have implemented ideas borrowed from the larger culture in order to grow. Let's focus on that.

The U.S. has been preoccupied with building self-esteem in its population for quite some time now. This trend contends that everyone is special and need not do anything but breathe the air. Everyone wins! There are no losers! Consequently, the U.S. has a large number of narcissistic people. Selfies, Facebook, Twitter (or any social media) and Reality TV: They all have, at their core, an excessive interest in the **self.** What people are saying with their ME! ME! ME! attitude is:

- *I am told that I am special early on.*
- *I win without accomplishing anything.*
- *I receive praise for just being here.*
- *I grow up receiving validation from others on a regular basis.*
- *I now need this external validation, because without it, I feel so empty inside.*

- *When I look into the mirror and don't know who I am, I demand that others hold up a mirror for me to gaze in.*
- *Social media is my mirror. Who I am rises or falls on how many Likes I get.*

This narcissistic attitude has infiltrated the churches. Many people walk through the doors of a church with a "What's in it for ME?" attitude. The goal of someone attending church in our modern age is not to gain maturity in the faith but to feel good about **myself.**

The goal of a church service in our modern age is not to foster maturity in the faith but to make the people feel good about **themselves.** Services consequently are emotional and experiential. No deep theology here; people need not really have a systematic understanding of that baneful book. The goal of church is feelings and only good feelings at that. Services are **Relevant! Relational! Really focused on YOU!**

Thus, when the "It's All About ME" folks walk into a church that is providing an "It's All About You!" atmosphere, we get a wonderful convergence: Perpetual baby christians who whine and cry about wanting to feel good and churches who bend over backward to wipe their noses and make them giggle. When do these babies grow up? They don't.

As soon as a pastor starts the heavy lifting of theology and "rightly dividing the Word of Truth," [19] many people pick up their binkies and blankies and head out the door, looking for a new "nursery."

Paul lamented our kind of church: "For the time will come when they will not endure sound doctrine; but wanting to have their ears tickled, they will accumulate for themselves teachers in accordance to their own desires, and will turn away their ears from the truth and will turn aside to myths."[20]

We loved that kind of church then and we keep promoting it today. So, the modern church, in its effort to keep people coming back, makes church services fun, hip, edgy, a kind of play-therapy, **not** (the Dark Lord forbid!) a deeply life-changing experience. Thoughts?

To: Baal-Kobalt <capturetheplanet@brimstone.com>

From: Wormwood <burnbabyburn@gothell.com>

Subject: Changin' diapers, not hearts

Hey BK! Another instructor of mine, Baal-Cholerat, taught us that in the Old Testament, when people went one-on-one with the enemy, they walked away changed.

You've got that Moses with the burning bush. That old shepherd could never go back to his sheep after that. He ended up becoming a shepherd to a whole nation, leading them to a land promised to his people long ago.

You've got that Elijah with the prophets of Baal. Baal worship back in the day was something to behold: lots of evil doin's. Elijah was a man on fire, calling it down on our priests and putting theirs out.

You've got that Isaiah when he encountered the enemy. POW! He realized just how sinful he and his people were. After that angel placed that coal on his tongue, he was burning to go out and speak for the enemy.

You've got that whiney Jeremiah who knew his words would be ignored. But he kept at the people, warning and telling them to get it together, for judgement was coming. They didn't want to hear it, of course, but that didn't stop him.

Once all those losers felt how big the enemy was, they also felt how big their sin was. But they all got a shot in the arm to go and stake a claim for the enemy. The New Testament folks were no different. When people finally understood who the enemy's son really was, they walked away changed as well. Those thick as a brick disciples eventually turned the world upside down.

That Peter, the I-Don't-Know-Him Guy, managed to bring 3000 people to the enemy's son with his first sermon. This guy, so ashamed before, turned into a powerhouse.

Even today (I'm bummed when I say this) a real one-on-one with the enemy's son means real change. When a person gets how big the enemy is and how big their sin is, they also get how much the enemy loves them. They turn around and walk to the enemy's beat. The ugliest caterpillar becomes a butterfly with the enemy in their life.

But, if your time with the enemy is just lots of cool feelings, then you can go in and out of his presence without any real sense of who he is. You, in turn, don't realize how sinful you are.

If you **feel** the need to repent (but not a gut-wrenching desire to do it) your turning away from sin is pretty shallow. You get all gushy inside and then give your life to the enemy. When your feelings wear off, so does your commitment to live for him.

To the enemy, it's all about changing the direction of your life: Away from sin and into the kind of life the enemy gives you power to live. That's what "repentance" means after all: makin' a U-turn from sin. But if your walk is all touchy-feely and not based on that book--'cause your church wants you happy not deep--you won't grow in the enemy. Just the way the Dark Lord likes it.

I dig the "yield" signs on life's interstate. I want to do road work in church, so lots of folks miss those U-turn signs, give up and yield.

> To: Wormwood <burnbabyburn@gothell.com>
>
> From: Baal-Kobalt <capturetheplanet@brimstone.com>
>
> Subject: Making faith irrelevant

You are so right. Or should I say, you are so right-a-way! (Resorting to your kind of playfulness will never do for a demon in my position.)

The enemy's son puts a constant emphasis on repentance. Sin is a barrier between the enemy and his children; he has always expended a lot of energy trying to overcome it and liberate his children.

Ever since Adam and Eve went into the Garden's produce section and got wisdom from us and not from him, the enemy has been on a constant rescue mission.

Whether it was the spilt blood of a lamb, a goat wandering out to die in the desert, a bronze serpent raised up on a pole over the people, or an offering consumed by fire, the enemy has always tried to impress upon his children the deadly serious nature of sin and the need for reconciliation between him and his children.

The enemy wants his children to turn from their wicked ways and be healed so they may return to his kingdom. The enemy's son even went so far as to die for sin—not only showing how serious it is, but also how much the enemy loves these soiled creatures. I find all of this utterly incomprehensible.

But, as we know, human beings want **the self** be their god. The self isn't interested in repentance. If some deluded human does enter the enemy's camp by walking into a church, we must see to it that the person will not be burdened with such ego-deflating concepts such as "hell," "sin," "repentance" and "disobedience" coming from the pastor or the church leadership.

These days, that fire and brimstone stuff is now as welcomed as a weasel in a henhouse. Today, it's about a more enlightened and friendly approach for those who are seeking:

- *It's not what you can do for the enemy, but what he can do for you!*
- *It's all about your prayers, your life, your happiness, your prosperity!*
- *Our focus? Your focus? You guessed it: you!*

It is interesting to note that the more broken society becomes, (the Dark Lord be praised!) the more people will wander into church focused on their unmet needs and shattered selves.

Well-intentioned pastors will then continue to create churches that are more like hospital wards than training camps. If everyone is lying in bed, no one is running missions to the gates of Hell.

If everyone is groaning about "What's in it for ME?!" then the cries of a lost world are not heard.

We must keep a person constantly focused on the self. We must keep church leaders accommodating this focus so the person will see the "benefits" of such a church and attend there. We see those "benefits" as well.

Let's listen in on a person going to our kind of church:

- *I go and gather with others, seeking a personal high, and not really connecting with a community of like-minded believers wanting to serve the Son. Church becomes a place for me to go in to and feel good about myself.*
- *I can compartmentalize my life. Here I am on Sunday, and there I am the rest of the week. I don't really let my faith interfere with how I live my life. I then go back to church, and having lived a double life, I seek to feel better. My conscience reminds me that I am not aligned with the biblical principles. But my pastor gives a happy sermon with stories and video clips. It lacks any real substance. It certainly doesn't encourage me to confront my sin. So, I am back in my happy place…for a while.*
- *I don't have to be accountable. I don't want to be accountable. I trump any comments about my lifestyle with the "We are not supposed to judge one another" card. I continue to live how I want.*
- *I go to church focused on me. I leave focused on me. I don't leave with a vibrant grow-in-the-knowledge-of-the-Lord kind of thing. All I take with me is an experience. I did not have a conviction for a deep life change.*

Here's where it gets really interesting for the Dark Kingdom. We watch as this person starts to think:

- *In the heat of life's battle, what knowledge I do have seems to evaporate.*
- *When I feel weak and face the week, life gets complicated and I don't know what to do.*
- *I am desperately looking for answers, so I become vulnerable to every wind of doctrine.*
- *I lose hope in what I have been taught, for it doesn't manage to stand up under pressure.*

- *Over time, I lose faith. I feel as if Heaven is not interested in me.*
- *Over time, I lose love. My heart turns away and I feel cold inside.*
- *Over time, I lose interest. There must be a better way than faith…*

That person's loss of all things heavenly is the Dark Kingdom's gain.

To: Baal-Kobalt <capturetheplanet@brimstone.com>

From: Wormwood <burnbabyburn@gothell.com>

Subject: The times, they ain't a-changin'

Hey BK! I can hear some fool whining: *Why do I go to church? To get my needs met!* Love it.

I can hear some fool church replying: *What is the point of our church service? To get your needs met!* Uh-huh.

This we-gotta-meet-your-needs kind of church will not preach that blasted book. Those in-your-face-about-sin parts make people feel bad about themselves. Can't do that!

Churches only use the book to support the culture's obsession with personal needs, fulfillment and purpose. We get a "user-friendly" gospel! But if you take away anything away from the gospel, it loses its power. Without power, no one is going to become like the enemy's son. The church just ends up rubber-stamping people's lives.

People's lives are a mess and sin-filled. The son and his word promise power and change for believers. The son wants to bring them life. Without pastors preaching that book from cover to cover, real power ain't flowing in the churches.

People walk in "as is," and people walk out "as is." Same 'ole thing, week after week.

The "What's in it for me?" church and the faith it presents has a simple answer: "Nothing."

Go ahead, Modern Church Leadership: Keep the gospel friendly, group-huggy and don't bash the culture. Make your church relevant! Relational! Experiential!

Go ahead, Mr. Modern Pastor…Forget what that traitor Paul said: "I am astonished that you are so quickly deserting the one who called you to live in the grace of Christ and are turning to a different gospel—which is really no gospel at all. Evidently some people are throwing you into confusion and are trying to pervert the gospel of Christ."[21]

Paul was such a party-pooper. Our Dark Lord preaches another gospel, and it suits me just fine. I have other choice words to describe Paul, but out of respect to you, BK, I'll chill.

> To: Wormwood <burnbabyburn@gothell.com>
>
> From: Baal-Kobalt <capturetheplanet@brimstone.com>
>
> Subject: No power? No problems!

Thank you. Respect for your superiors will keep you from being transformed into a boil on the backside of a politician.

Another benefit of preaching a diluted gospel is when people are not experiencing the enemy's life-transforming power (that nauseating "abundant life" the enemy's son promised) they must redefine sin to accommodate it. If people are not overcoming such and such sin, then perhaps the sin is not really a problem! It's who they **are.** You don't try to change a zebra into a horse, do you? They rename the sin a "lifestyle" or consider it "genetic." People are then "survivors," **not** "overcomers" as that boastful book asserts.

The son's power is not there in such a church to change lives. Consequently, people assume that being affirming and happy is the only realistic goal of the church and what it does.

With no power and no changed lives, people come to see faith as overrated or desperately needing to be redefined. The church becomes more a social club or a convalescent ward, filled with people who are just trying to get along in this life. This kind of church is slowly submerging under the cultural tide. As someone once observed, "Those who stand for nothing will fall for everything."

This kind of church will be easily commandeered by those who will follow our Man of Action's progressive program. When he strides onto the scene and grabs the culture by the throat, the church will also choke.

To: Baal-Kobalt <capturetheplanet@brimstone.com>

From: Wormwood <burnbabyburn@gothell.com>

Subject: If it's all about you, ditch others

Hey BK! All of those words spoken by the enemy's son on serving one another gets thrown under the bus when "It's all about ME!" People certainly want others to be concerned for them. Return the favor? Nah. 'Cause it's all about you.

Serving means getting outside yourself, but a church with a "you focus" doesn't grow servants, but selfies. People feel alone in church, because no one connects or cares. That "Body of Christ" stuff gets forgotten. People who follow the son are to stick together. But if we keep the drumbeat of "you, you, you," then why hang out with others?

I watch for those lonely christians, wandering down life's highway. Why? I drive a semi.

> To: Wormwood <burnbabyburn@gothell.com>
> From: Baal-Kobalt <capturetheplanet@brimstone.com>
> Subject: Making Jesus a Big Mac

Spiritual road-kill. Such a delicious thought. Let us move on to another trend that has infiltrated the church.

When narcissism meets consumerism, we get a potent brew.

In an effort to make church more accessible to the "unchurched," many well-intentioned pastors decided to "market" (although they would never use that word) their churches in a more "user-friendly" way.

Churches used all sorts of ways to make services more accessible and friendly to those with little or no church background. A church-goer became more of a consumer, or a customer, if you will. It became the church's job to present a more palatable product to keep the customer interested and coming back for more.

So, the enemy's son became a spiritual Big Mac.

Ever had one, my fusty demon? Nothing offensive about that burger. The meat is rather bland, and the only interesting thing is the sauce. Millions love it! Why? **Because it is tasty enough to be attractive but not forceful enough in flavor to turn people off.**

That's exactly how we want the church to present the enemy's son. Make the enemy's son attractive by emphasizing his unconditional love, his acceptance, his tolerance. Drop his forceful teachings on morality, personal sacrifice and self-discipline. Many churches today have obliged us in this. We must keep this trend going.

I must digress, but only for a moment. That "unconditional love" business needs to be constantly thrown into confusion by us. The son on the cross went unconditionally, dying for those who didn't even know or care about him. He went solely out of love. But, keep that "unconditional" part regarding the believer deliberately unclear. Make it sound as if there are no standards to keep, no walking in obedience or no living a life that reflects the son's power being expressed through his followers. "Unconditional love" becomes synonymous with "Live it because he'll forgive it."

The enemy's son talked about how his followers need to daily pick up their cross. By doing that, a person shows, out of their love for the enemy, a willingness to follow the son, deny the self and die to sin. The way we can subvert this is to encourage light and superficial teaching from the pulpit, with little or no use of that book.

The modern church's cross is Styrofoam: it looks good, but lacks any substance.

| To: Baal-Kobalt <capturetheplanet@brimstone.com> |
| From: Wormwood <burnbabyburn@gothell.com> |
| Subject: Not just a Big Mac, but a Big Me! |

Hey BK! If humans turn Jesus into something different than what that book says, they're making him into an idol. Yup: An idol—a god who makes humans feel good.

Remember what that kill-joy Paul said? "But even if we or an angel from heaven should preach a gospel other than the one we preached to you, let them be under God's curse! As we have already said, so now I say again: If anybody is preaching to you a gospel other than what you accepted, let them be under God's curse!"[22]

Is Paul mocking the Dark Lord's time as the beautiful angel, Lucifer? Ticks me off.

Anyway, humans now don't go for wood or stone idols, but they still love having something or someone they can create and then control. Baal-Tyrannus taught us that idols are gods humans can control with what they do and think. It's a "Hey! I obey you, so now you need to do what I want!" kind of thing.

The enemy wants humans to serve him out of love and respect. But that yanks humans right out of the driver's seat. Idols work 'cause humans love to grab the wheel and hit the gas!

What to do? Teach a Jesus who's all about today's values. He is tolerant, non-judgmental, and comfortable. He's **modern.** He's the perfect product for the modern church-shopper! Or, create a Jesus who's kinda like everybody!

You can just hear the modern church shopper thinkin':

- *I want a Jesus who is better than me, somewhat, but not too good! I have to relate to him. If he is too good, then the standards for my behavior would have to go up.*
- *If he's not too good, I can respect him. He's like me.*
- *If I can't find a church with such a Jesus, I'll just keep a-church-shoppin' until I do. I don't want accountability.*
- *I want no worries. I'm just a smart shopper.*

I do like that Styrofoam cross idea—even that beggar Paul reminds the believers to choose carefully the kinds of materials they build with as they follow the son: "For no one can lay any foundation other than the one already laid, which is Jesus Christ. If anyone builds on this foundation using gold, silver, costly stones, wood, hay or straw, their work will be shown for what it is, because the Day will bring it to light. It will be revealed with fire, and the fire will test the quality of each person's work."[23]

Here's my building materials list I love to hand off to the son's followers:

- ✓ Styrofoam Spirituality (light, no heavy lifting)
- ✓ Pride Trusses (they hold up until the going gets tough)
- ✓ Plastic Piety Wrap (stretches to fit all circumstances)
- ✓ Deceit Drywall (covers a multitude of sins)
- ✓ Happy Paint (one coat is all you need to cover the stony heart underneath)

WW's Home Improvement Store sells nothing but the finest! Those are the kinds of materials I love believers to work with. When those materials get tested by fire someday, we will have ringside seats to a smokin' show!

To: Wormwood <burnbabyburn@gothell.com>

From: Baal-Kobalt <capturetheplanet@brimstone.com>

Subject: The joy of idolatry

We will enjoy s'mores together on that Day. Let us continue.

Idols will never leave the scene because of human pride. Humans so love to be the ones in control of their lives. If they stay out of that book, then they can create the next generation's Jesus. Their pride says: *We will get him right—other generations did not understand him as we moderns do. Our new church will reflect that new reality!*

If the blasted book doesn't drive belief, then pride will. What's wrong with pride anyway? The Dark Lord was so beautiful in His younger days. Why not have pride in that? Why not try to rule heaven? He was certainly qualified. He was an angel of light. Why do you think so many of his fellow angels went with him when he was so unfairly exiled?

But, as you mentioned, because our Dark Lord couldn't usurp the enemy's position, He went after the next best thing: those maggoty children of his.

Pride operating in the human heart says: *This God-thing is overrated, and I need to assert control.*

Pride operating in the church heart says: *Old-school church is just that—we need a Jesus who will keep bringing modern people back. It's our job to get them through the doors. We don't want to offend or drive people off, so keep the focus on meeting needs, and use the Bible to encourage people, not exhort them.*

So, off to McChurch we go! Allowing consumerism to influence churches has resulted in such delightful developments. "Success" is now measured by huge church buildings, lots of programs, and lots of folks in the pews. Success means blessed. These churches equate blessings only with material prosperity. **They walk by sight, not by faith.**

A business measures success by how many products it sells. If I build a car that practically everyone wants to own, and sell a huge number, then I would call my car company "successful." Whether or not the car is a quality car is not the issue; it is how many I sell. Now, of course, the car will have to have some kind of quality in it. An obvious piece of junk won't sell. But if I can market my car cleverly, and entice people to buy it without having them look too closely, then I will be successful. Sales equal money, and in a consumer-driven country like the U.S., money is seen as the hallmark of success.

We must continue applying this idea to church where bigger is seen as blessed. This is a marvelous way to dilute the gospel's power and influence in the lives of believers. Then christianity as a whole loses its influence throughout the U.S. The biblical definition of success is not measured by filling a huge church up every Sunday morning. It is building an army of believers who walk as the enemy's son walked. These dedicated soldiers run missions against the Gates of Hell. Again and again.

Let's keep **that definition** of success out of sight.

To: Baal-Kobalt <capturetheplanet@brimstone.com>

From: Wormwood <burnbabyburn@gothell.com>

Subject: The U.S.' god is green!

Hey BK! Yeah, that book talks of material blessings but for many christians, that's the only kind. The enemy's creation should bless the socks off every believer. But his creation, mercy and grace (gag!) lose their meaning in a "God-Wants-**Success**-for-ME!" environment. The modern church is living out "bigger is blessed." But, if the "customer" is always right, then pastors got a problem.

The "Word of God" is just that—the enemy's words aimed at sinful humans. We, of course, would prefer it to be the "Word of Man," because then all churches would be our kind of church, with no guts and no Glory!

But, if pastors preach that book in all of its no-nonsense, in-your-face and "the truth will set you free" kind of way (ugh!) then the consumer might not "like" the "product" and leave.

How did that traitor Paul put it? "For the preaching of the cross is to them that perish foolishness; but unto us which are saved it is the power of God."[24]

How to keep that success bus rolling? Pastors must be encouraged to cherry-pick only those passages in that book which make the customer/church-goer happy. Don't preach those verses on divorce, immorality (at least don't get too specific) death to self, discipline, and the daily carrying of your cross. The message must be light and hip, keepin' the sheep happy.

If a pastor ticks off "customers" who bring in the bucks, who's gonna pay the bills for that ginormous church?

Replace the Bread of Life with Spiritual Fast Food. Turn Jesus into a Big Mac. Make church a "drive-thru" experience: a quick order, a quick meal of little spiritual value and a smile as you leave. No substance. No calls to holiness. No fruit showing a changed life.

Results of McChurch? Its customers will continue to return. Its bills will continue to get paid. Its impact on people and the culture? **What impact?**

To: Wormwood <burnbabyburn@gothell.com>
From: Baal-Kobalt <capturetheplanet@brimstone.com>
Subject: Shake it to break it

Indeed. The best way to marginalize christianity in the U.S. is to render it powerless from within. If the assault comes openly from the outside, christians will unite against the common foe. But, drain christianity of its vitality in the churches and it loses its validity.

What do I mean by that? If the central claim of christianity is to transform the believer into the image of the enemy's son and that is not really happening, then people start to question its validity and truthfulness of its teachings.

Its truth is directly associated with that book: "So then faith cometh by hearing, and hearing by the word of God."[25]

That book is essential to this process: "And be not conformed to this world: but be ye transformed by the renewing of your mind, that ye may prove what is that good, and acceptable, and perfect, will of God."[26]

But, if the focus shifts to making the church comfortable to those coming in, then that book will be set aside more and more. So, too, will the enemy's power to change lives, as we have observed.

It is disgusting how powerful that book is: "For the word of God is quick, and powerful, and sharper than any two edged sword, piercing even to the dividing asunder of soul and spirit, and of the joints and marrow, and is a discerner of the thoughts and intents of the heart."[27]

Less of that book and people will grow more dissatisfied with their faith and The Faith.

Faith will become less powerful over time because of increasing compromise. To compensate for the loss of real change in people's lives, churches will want to create a more human-affirming set of beliefs and remake the church into their own image. This kind of progressive church will reflect *their* values and aspirations.

If the enemy's Spirit left most churches today, would anyone even notice? I doubt it.

> To: Baal-Kobalt <capturetheplanet@brimstone.com>
>
> From: Wormwood <burnbabyburn@gothell.com>
>
> Subject: Ask not what you can do for God, but what God can do for YOU!

Hey BK! Yup, we gotta water down that book! Water down the message! Then ditto for the enemy's power!

The whole disgusting goal is laid out by that traitor Paul: "And we all, who with unveiled faces contemplate the Lord's glory, are being transformed into his image with ever-increasing glory, which comes from the Lord…"[28]

I liked Paul better when he was smiling over dead christians back in the day. Paul became ugly once he went over to the enemy's side. He did quite a bit of damage to the Dark Kingdom. Paul's total change from slay-er to pray-er shows what the enemy can do when someone is all in.

The less churches teach Paul, along with a blander gospel, the better off the Dark Kingdom. Hey, speaking of that traitor Paul, I need to be clear on something that Baal-Tarneesh taught us many years ago about this "born-again" nonsense. Humans can't really be born again, can they?

> To: Wormwood <burnbabyburn@gothell.com>
>
> From: Baal-Kobalt <capturetheplanet@brimstone.com>
>
> Subject: Service with a wile

Let me state categorically that the more misunderstood this "new creation" or "born-again" teaching is, the more we can search and destroy such incursions by the enemy in the heart of a believer.

The enemy's son along with Paul and his writings are a huge stumbling stone to us, but in order to subvert a teaching, you need to first understand it.

Let me also remind you that in the McChurch, systematic theology is tantamount to yelling "Shark!" at a seaside resort. People can't get out of there fast enough. You are getting the information that churches used to teach, but they've set it aside now for more dynamic sermons.

We encourage pastors to be hip, go to the Internet, download a sermon and away we go. You don't have to sit at the enemy's feet, listening for his word to the people. You don't need to have a deep relationship with the enemy, because the church exists to create a happy atmosphere, which, in turn, creates happy "customers." Thus, the word/Word to the church is happy, easy, lightweight and geared to please. No more teaching a systematic understanding of that book. Just a verse here and there.

Just enough for people **to think** they know that book. Under fire, such folks wither.

So, when our "gotta earn your way into heaven" types knock on the door, these bible-lite folks don't know what to say. No one is the wiser. The "gotta earn it" types only listen to their authorities about what that book means (not reading it for themselves).

The wide-eyed ones opening the door can't navigate through that book to defend it if their lives depended on it. Well, maybe not their life. But their eternal life? That's an entirely new conversation.

So, good question, my inquiring minded WW. You actually show more curiosity about spiritual matters than many of the enemy's so-called children. What are you trying to understand exactly?

> To: Baal-Kobalt <capturetheplanet@brimstone.com>
> From: Wormwood <burnbabyburn@gothell.com>
> Subject: The New Man?

Hey BK! OK, here goes. Paul talks about a second Adam. I like the first Adam 'cause he was stupid. Adam got it direct from the enemy not to eat from that Tree. What'd he go and do? He listened to Eve, took the fruit (the bait?) and committed the big cosmic no-no.

"He sinned, she sinned and we winned!" was Baal-Tarneesh's rallying cry.

In fact, at Evil Academy, we'd have a Fall 'N' Fruit Festival, and pelt each other with apples on campus. Some demon got to act out the Adam-being-stupid part. One of the Baals, of course, acted out our Dark Lord's part. One year, it was hard to find a snake costume to fit Baal-LaGauche, because he is one big demon. He did a great job though, hissing at Adam. Taunting him. Making the enemy's "wonderful" (yeah, right) creation look about as safe as a zebra ordering out at Dandy-Lion's Pizza Parlor.

The ending of the performance was my favorite part: A huge container of poop opened up overhead, and dumped a ton on top of "Adam's" head! Such a perfect ending to the idea that Adam was somehow special. Nah. Just full of crap. (What that book calls "sin.") But then here comes Paul, with all this yak-yak about a second Adam. I was taught we tagged and bagged the first one!

> To: Wormwood <burnbabyburn@gothell.com>
> From: Baal-Kobalt <capturetheplanet@brimstone.com>
> Subject: Paul's turd-y teaching in our punchbowl

Let us go directly to the source of this pernicious teaching about Adam and Jesus: "So it is written: 'The first man Adam became a living being;' the last Adam, a life-giving spirit." [29]

Ergo, the Second Adam is the enemy's son, who came to give his followers not just life, but a new life. The son is called "the last Adam." That implies he came to create a new kind of Adam on the earth, a new kind of man, filled with the power of the enemy's son.

Think of it this way: When the enemy set out to create humans, he shaped the ground into a human form, and then breathed in his "breath of life" into it, and the soul of man became alive. We were not pleased.

Once Adam decided to listen to us and not to the enemy, sin entered this ridiculous planet and tainted everything. Creation as well as humanity fell under what that book call the "curse."

We called it the "Fortunate Fall." We got in to the enemy's house, his creation, and we don't plan to leave anytime soon. I know the enemy thinks otherwise. But then here comes the son. The son goes to the cross, pays the debt incurred by Adam and then walks out of that tomb. He breathes his life into man, and puts to death that old sin nature (Adam's gift to humanity) and creates a new man with a new nature (the son's gift to humanity).

This new nature wants to please and serve the enemy. The enemy is showing again how much he wants to take this planet back and to set free our captives.

We fight vigorously to prevent someone from accepting this new life from the son. With the son, a person has hope and the power to walk in freedom. A person soon realizes what our work really is in their lives: captivity.

We must constantly reemphasize that we offer **real** freedom. We tell the person that *Hey! Do what you want, when you want, and have no regrets!*

When we tap into that sin nature, our suggestions have a ring of truth to them.

But when someone accepts the son, and his new life come bursting forth out of the believer's heart, we are in trouble. Suddenly that lush banquet set out by the Dark Kingdom for the enemy's children seems unappetizing and unappealing.

Oh, of course, we work aggressively to lure them back to the table, but the sheep hear another voice. They seem to not only know this shepherd, but actually want to follow him.

It's appalling to be sure, but that's why we do what we do. That baneful book says that we come to destroy, kill and take whatever we want. Its assessment of our mission is very accurate.

To: Baal-Kobalt <capturetheplanet@brimstone.com>

From: Wormwood <burnbabyburn@gothell.com>

Subject: Retreading the old Adam?

Hey BK! Sounds kinda weird that human beings can really change. Yeah, they go to some church service, get all emotionally wound up and then go to the altar, tears streaming down their stupid faces, and kneeling with a desire to get right with the son.

Isn't the enemy just gilding a turd? Isn't he just putting some new rubber on an old tire?

The enemy's son taught that the seeds he sows get either taken up by us, scorched by the world, or strangled by worry.

I am not a math whizz, but that leaves only about a quarter of the seeds that he casts taking root and becoming a threat to the Dark Kingdom. Pretty low return. How can those 25% live the life the son calls them to?

> To: Wormwood <burnbabyburn@gothell.com>
>
> From: Baal-Kobalt <capturetheplanet@brimstone.com>
>
> Subject: Baptized, buried and brought to life

Not a re-tread, my demon, but a whole new set of tires from on high to roll down that holy road.

The son taught about new wine in new wineskins. It's not about recycling the old stuff or putting new life into an old human. It's about a new inside, a new man, a new creation, a new birth. Let's again focus on Paul. It's a long quote, but for you to understand how the enemy thinks, you must hear his words:

"We know that our old sinful selves were crucified with Christ so that sin might lose its power in our lives. We are no longer slaves to sin. For when we died with Christ we were set free from the power of sin. And since we died with Christ, we know we will also live with him. We are sure of this because Christ was raised from the dead, and he will never die again. Death no longer has any power over him. When he died, he died once to break the power of sin. But now that he lives, he lives for the glory of God. So you also should consider yourselves to be dead to the power of sin and alive to God through Christ Jesus..."[30]

Do you see? The believer is baptized, crucified and resurrected with the son. That's what that born-again nonsense means in a nutshell. Let me emphasize the "nut" part of that.

Why is the enemy so willing to rescue these maggots? It is truly a mystery to me. The believer is thus a new creation, created from the son's obedience to the will of his father: the son was willing to die on behalf of a fallen humanity. Sin's debt had to be paid by the shedding of blood. The son willingly offered himself.

I must say that we did our best to make his last days on this wretched planet as agonizing as possible. Crucifixion is such a dark delight. Everyone gets to watch, and the pain of the person on that cross defies description. We laughed through and with the Romans. We dropped idea after idea into their puny minds, helping the son suffer endlessly. (We really loved the crown of thorns bit. Such a mighty king with blood dripping into his eyes.) We wanted to make his death so horrible that his followers would run away and never return.

We never saw the resurrection coming. Who could have predicted that? Death is our most potent weapon and the finality of it makes the Dark Kingdom roar with delight. That Sunday morning still rankles His Dark Majesty. The enemy's son was able to push right past death, right past that stone and reappear in his glory.

We so regretted that Sunday. We had so much fun that Friday.

Now, because of that empty cross and empty tomb, the son's very life is breathed into the person who accepts him. The enemy's son is the new "ground" from which the new man is made. Adam was made from the dust; followers of the son are made from the son's sacrifice. Idiot Paul declares: "So now there is no condemnation for those who belong to Christ Jesus... And because you belong to him, the power of the life-giving Spirit has freed you from the power of sin that leads to death..."[31]

The enemy's son inaugurated a new law when he rose from the dead. The Law from Moses couldn't save humanity—it just made them either want to sin more (the forbidden is always alluring) or made them feel that they could never measure up. We kept harping on both points every generation. But then Paul had the gall to assert that the enemy handed down a new law because of the son's death on the cross: The son now lives in the believer, living his life through him.

We find that about as useful as a fly swatter in a spaceship.

If the enemy's son is now living inside the believer, he provides the power to live the life that he asks of his children. In return, the enemy receives what he desires: restored and continuing fellowship with his children. In our estimation, this is a detestable state of affairs, to be sure.

That rat Paul says, "I have been crucified with Christ; and it is no longer I who live, but Christ lives in me; and the life which I now live in the flesh I live by faith in the son of God, who loved me and gave Himself up for me."[32]

My only consolation to all of this is I had a front row seat when the Roman guard wacked off that beggar's head after his trial in Rome. I thought I saw a smile on his face, though. Did Paul know something we don't?

To: Baal-Kobalt <capturetheplanet@brimstone.com>

From: Wormwood <burnbabyburn@gothell.com>

Subject: Yeah, that grace garbage gets old

Hey BK! Another one of my instructors, Baal-Acide, once commented that we blew it when we nailed the enemy's son to that cross. Paul mocked us by saying if we had only known, we wouldn't have "crucified the Lord of glory."[33]

Yup. That day was a train wreck for the Dark Kingdom.

It's that grace thing again. The enemy wanted to restore what was lost in the Garden. So he tried again and again with Moses' Law, the temple sacrifices, and all that blood as a covering. The enemy's love message didn't click with those maggoty humans. Finally, his son took up the charge. He gave himself to die on that cross. I get it: Now he gives himself to each believer, living his life through them. Yuck.

Humans just aren't worth all this bother. They are a blast to torment, but to save them? No way.

The enemy's plan is to save humans **from** the fires of hell. We save them **for** the fires of hell.

> To: Wormwood <burnbabyburn@gothell.com>
> From: Baal-Kobalt <capturetheplanet@brimstone.com>
> Subject: I had to save YOU, you big-mouthed demon!

Never, ever remind us of our miscalculations regarding the son and his mission to earth. My delay in getting back to you was I received an order from the Center of Hell to have you immediately eliminated. I argued persuasively (you are still here, correct?) that all of the training you have received would be wasted if you were turned into a pile of smoking ash.

Our miscalculations were regrettable, yes. But we never look back. We only look forward to the Hell we will raise, especially before the son returns.

Ever since that Sunday morning, we have never stopped tormenting the son's followers. We tried to eliminate those twelve disciples as soon as we could. Judas was just too easy. We managed to release the full fury of hell on them, except for that beggar John.

John being whisked off to the island of Patmos was not acceptable to us. The Center of Hell sent out numerous directives to eliminate him. Not only did John survive, but he received a powerful revelation of the End Times and recorded what he saw. He foresaw our Man of Action, leading the battle that will unleash the Dark Kingdom's forces in all their gory and glory against the enemy's forces.

Every generation of the son's followers set their hope on the son's return. They act as if we have lost, thanks in no small part to that traitor John and his "revelation." More like a "revulsion" to us.

We know how the story ends. Way back in the Garden we had it thrown in our faces as the enemy denounced us. Those words about our Dark Lord's head being crushed still gall us. But His Darkness will continue to bruise the son's heel every chance He gets.

Conduct yourself, however, in all obedience to the Dark Kingdom and speak only of its goals, gains and glory. If you cannot do this, I won't be responsible for the consequences.

To: Baal-Kobalt <capturetheplanet@brimstone.com>

From: Wormwood <burnbabyburn@gothell.com>

Subject: Way sorry!

Hey BK! Whoa! I meant no disrespect to the Dark Kingdom. Thank you for going to bat for me. Whew. I am glad I missed another bullet. I'd hate to see how someone gets eliminated when the Center of Hell gets involved. Shiver.

One more question, OK? So, the son lives his life through his followers in the same way we live through our followers? The only difference may be that our followers don't always know that we are using them to do the Dark Kingdom's work.

The enemy's followers have fellowship with him. We have hell-o-ship with ours.

I guess the spirit world has to have hands and feet to get things done, whether it's for the enemy's kingdom or ours.

I am so glad I play on the team I do. We have Auschwitz, Hiroshima, 9/11, human trafficking, terrorism, slavery and murder to our credit. The enemy's kingdom? Hospitals, orphanages, relief groups and adoption. Big whoop-di-do.

We get the fun stuff.

To: Wormwood <burnbabyburn@gothell.com>

From: Baal-Kobalt <capturetheplanet@brimstone.com>

Subject: Counterfeit

We do not possess bodies. We are grateful for that of course. We don't have to bother with death or decay. In order to do the work we are commissioned to do by our Dark Lord on this repugnant planet, we must take up residence in the heart and mind of a human.

Let me draw you an analogy. In ancient times, humans built cities encompassed by large, imposing walls. The walls had gates in them, which were opened to allow traffic in and out. At night, or at times of warfare or other dangers, the gates were locked.

The human being's heart and mind is like that ancient city, enclosed by a wall of the will. If a person chooses to honor the son, in thought and deed, we can pound on the gates through temptation, trying to get that person to open up. If the gates are locked, heart and mind are safe.

But if this person decides to open the gates, we rejoice and come in, creating chaos. But if that person resists, those gates remain locked. That blasted book is a sure-fire way to keep a person's heart and mind safe and keeping the will locked against our incursions, because it informs, encourages and empowers a follower to do so.

The person can keep the "city" safe by fellowshipping with other believers, engaging in heart-felt worship, pursuing avid prayer and having such a deep relationship with the son that the person hears his voice. This person is walking in the enemy's spirit.

We never cease trying to get a person to open up those gates. As you well know, you seek out a person's vulnerability, and hit that hard. If the person opens the gates just a little, perhaps out of curiosity, we can move in. The sound of the latch being opened and the creaking of the hinges is music to the Dark Kingdom's ears.

But, if a small seemingly "innocent" temptation can't open the gates, we escalate. We tempt with drugs, alcohol, porn and other addictive enticements calculated to ensnare a person's will. Once the gates swing wide open, we are free to go in and out, bringing in more and more suggestions on how to go deeper and deeper into sin.

The Dark Kingdom regards the son's way as a counterfeit to ours. Here's how the enemy does it: The son enters into the gates when asked to do so by the person. He lives in the heart and directs the mind with his words. He guides the person with his voice, and grows the person in the knowledge and ways of the enemy's kingdom. He imitates us in that he gives the person power and insight to live the life he desires the person to live.

The biggest difference is the son is very willing to forgive any sin. He greatly desires that the person live in his strength and in his provision only, giving less and less attention to what that book calls "the flesh."

We argue with the person to not seek forgiveness. We show the person the benefits of sin. We downplay it:

- *Your sin was not that bad!*
- *You didn't hurt anyone!*
- *Your sin was not as bad as that other guy's sin!*

We also downplay the consequences, so the person sins again and again. Only later do those trespasses turn into a toxic brew, slowly but surely poisoning the person. Our unspoken goal with every sin, big or small, hidden or overt, is to eventually destroy the person, body and soul. (An added benefit to us: The more a person can lead others into sin and destruction, the more we pester that person, knowing how much they can help us in our work.)

We then start the endgame:

- *You are way too far gone for any forgiveness!*
- *You are a worthless person!*
- *Your shame is what you deserve!*
- *Your guilt is what you deserve!*
- *You might as well dive in deep, because you are past redemption!*
- *There are lots of ways to deaden your conscience! Go to it!*

We give knowledge to our followers. We give them insight. We give them power to do mighty things on our Dark Lord's behalf. Best of all, we come in and use people to engage in all sorts of victories for the Dark Kingdom. Oh, excuse me; humans call these events "atrocities."

We need an army. The enemy needs an army. The spirit world will go out and find who is open and use that person for its ends. The person will either honor the Dark Lord or the enemy. Humans have a choice. We love to corrupt that choice, and have a person open the gates to **us.** Our enticements are endless. The enemy uses love to encourage the person to open the gates to him and his forgiveness and power are endless.

The battle for the person's heart and mind will only end on the deathbed. Until then, we fight. Until then, the enemy fights. Our endgame? Destruction, death in life and death after death. The enemy's endgame? Life in life and life after death.

We need to move on. Are you satisfied with what I have taught you?

To: Baal-Kobalt <capturetheplanet@brimstone.com>

From: Wormwood <burnbabyburn@gothell.com>

Subject: I'm good

Hey BK! I guess it all boils down to that day in the Garden. Our Dark Lord sparked Eve's curiosity, questioned the enemy's words and then lured her to think that there was a better way to live. Of course, the really bad consequence was far into the future. Adam and Eve didn't physically die for a long time after that. Spiritually? Dead as a coffin nail.

They had to pay Hell in the meantime with getting kicked out of the Garden, pulling up weeds and burying Abel. Physical death took a while to show up.

When a human opens the gates, we should come in like a lamb. Save the lion stuff for later, where we chow down on a person's soul. **Keep it light and easy—at first:**

- A person has a drink now and then, but soon that person can't go anywhere without having a drink. DUI's, affairs, domestic violence, and child abuse are all done under alcohol's nasty influence. Keep the drinking fun as long as you can! (But the bad stuff will show up…someday.)
- A person takes an occasional glance at porn on the computer but soon that person can't go a day without having a look. Those images will take over and the person's mind is busy, busy, busy. For now, make the person thinks it's all under control! (But it degrades the soul and relationships over time…)
- A person goes to lunch with an attractive co-worker but soon that person is thinking about having more than a lunch date. Marriage, family and self-respect will all fly out the window. But, for now, it's safe—nothing has happened yet! (I love the "yet.")

We never advertise sin for what it is: slavery to us! We advertise it as fun. Despite our ad campaign getting exposed by the son, humans still fall for it.

The son is always offering to help the person get out of the pit that we help set up: "He lifted me out of the pit of despair, out of the mud and the mire. He set my feet on solid ground and steadied me as I walked along."[34]

But, if we keep that book on the shelves of a person's life, gathering dust, we can hammer that person once they fall into that pit:

- *No forgiveness! You're beyond the enemy's reach!*
- *No one loves you! You'll never come out of this!*

- *You are a loser! No one will miss you if you leave!*
- *Why don't you just end it all?*

Wow. Being a demon is so much fun. You know, so what if that Revelation book by that idiot John says we lose. Let's raise Hell and have fun in the meantime! Party on! Got it. I am ready now to move on to how we can mess up the churches and all those dumb sheep who stumble into them week after week.

> To: Wormwood <burnbabyburn@gothell.com>
>
> From: Baal-Kobalt <capturetheplanet@brimstone.com>
>
> Subject: Gutting prayer

Good. We know you are an enthusiastic demon. Keep that attitude in the days to come. We will need daredevils (pun intended!) like you all over this country to implement our agenda.

If church is where humans meet the enemy, and that environment is compromised by diluting that stumbling stone of a book, we have a stronger influence over the churches, as we have discussed. We need to equally undermine how humans talk to the enemy. Let's examine prayer.

If the church is encouraged to be driven by feelings, so should prayer be as well. If the people in the church are kept as babies by keeping that book "user-friendly," (uncomplicated and non-confrontational) their feelings will stay infantile. By keeping the believers immature in all aspects of their walk, their prayers will be no different.

We encourage church leaders to make the enemy into the kind of god people **want, not need.** People should be nudged **to pray answers, not requests**. Thus, if the answer doesn't come down exactly as the person prayed it, we can sow doubt into the person's faith. Our ultimate goal is to belittle prayer and ultimately (much to our delight) the enemy himself.

The prayers should be an extension of the self: *My way, my goals, my...my...my...It all begins and ends with ME!* Undermine the enemy's prerogative. Present him as willing/needing to do humans' bidding. Oh, and that "Thy will be done" business? Make believers shake and shiver with that one. Remind them that the last time someone prayed that, he went up on a cross.

Harp on unanswered prayer. "Unanswered" can be anything from:

- *You didn't do what I wanted!*
- *Why didn't this or that change?*
- *Why did that person suffer and die?*

Death is such an effective nail in the coffin of faith. In McChurch, remember, it's a "drive-thru" experience—you place your order (prayer) and expect it (the answer) waiting for you as you leave. Services with a smile: from the church and from the enemy. Simple and carefree.

Keep the person focused only on prayers where the challenges outweigh the answers: a sick person suffers with chronic pain with no relief in sight; a person loses a job and the long unemployment causes savings to dwindle; a person is spiritually confused and never seems to receive an answer.

We assist in diminishing gratitude to the enemy by distracting the person's attention away from the enemy's daily provisions. Daily bread is upstaged by a sick family member who doesn't seem to be getting better, despite all that praying.

But, remember, in the McChurch, consumers want more! They want better! They want **upgrades!** So, if the enemy finally provides a job but not a good paying job, or he provides a house, but not a big house, foster discontentment by emphasizing what a pitiful answer to prayer that was!

Despite all the prayers for healing, if the person dies, don't let the family see it as release from earthly bonds to a place of peace. Make them angry at the enemy! Help them to believe that now this person has passed, they cannot go on. Help them to believe that the enemy could have done more, but did not.

We so delight in these lies.

> To: Baal-Kobalt <capturetheplanet@brimstone.com>
>
> From: Wormwood <burnbabyburn@gothell.com>
>
> Subject: Count your disappointments, not your blessings

Hey BK! Yup, that ugly book nails it: "Look after each other so that none of you fails to receive the grace of God. Watch out that no poisonous root of bitterness grows up to trouble you, corrupting many."[35]

If we can keep the believer's focus on unanswered prayers and not on the enemy's mercy and grace, we can hammer home how useless prayer really is. Just keep passin' the bitter bottle, so the enemy's children keep takin' a swig. The more people stop talking to the enemy, the more likely they are to listen to us. We've got lots of way to get people to listen to us: the media, the culture, the schools and yes, the churches.

> To: Wormwood <burnbabyburn@gothell.com>
> From: Baal-Kobalt <capturetheplanet@brimstone.com>
> Subject: Make faith itself an idol

Well said. Another tactic we can use to undermine the church is to turn faith itself into a kind of idol. Make sure the person praying gets focused on how much faith they have, and not on the relationship they have with the enemy. Make sure the person believes that with enough faith, the enemy must answer.

Not only does this faith-hoarding give the person a false sense of control—*Look at my faith everyone!*—but it also morphs into a burden. What started out as--*Look at my faith! God will answer my prayers!*--can, over time, turn into--*Uh-oh, I didn't have enough faith and that's why this terrible thing happened!*

Either way, the character of the enemy is called into question. Prayer is called into question. Faith becomes a burden. Misrepresent prayer as dependent on what a person **does**. Faith-hoarding is a kind of "doing" and is also a way for a person to exert control over a situation. (We know that it's a false control, but humans love it nonetheless.)

By making faith into a kind of idol, a person feels empowered: not by faith in the enemy **but by faith in faith.**

Instead of believers trusting the enemy to do what's best, the "name it, claim it and frame it" kind of faith provides such fertile ground for disappointment in believers' lives. The enemy will be seen as not honoring that abundance of faith.

Such disappointment may even lead to the destruction of their faith altogether. It also turns a church into a place where

Job's friends would feel right at home. Everyone is staring and silently sneering at the person who is still struggling with unanswered prayers: *That won't happen to me. I have enough faith, unlike so-and-so.*

People start to even shun such a person. The person senses the condemnation and starts to isolate away from church. Instead of the church being the body of the son, it becomes the bullring. We love to cheer at such events.
The enemy's son's said that he came to give abundant life. We come to give abundant death.

This dovetails nicely into my favorite subject: suffering. Any comments first?

To: Baal-Kobalt <capturetheplanet@brimstone.com>

From: Wormwood <burnbabyburn@gothell.com>

Subject: Keeping people's faith off-kilter

Hey BK: Humans love to go to one extreme or another. Believers aren't any different. They do this "all or nothing" thinking as well. It's hard for people to get balanced and keep it. I've seen lots of folks go one way or another. You bet I helped. "Go big or go home!" is what I say! Here's what I whisper to pester believers to go to one side or the other:

- *Ramp up your faith to show the son how much you've got! He'll have to listen!* **Or...***Faith doesn't matter and you can't really do anything because the enemy is the only one pulling the strings, and no one can figure him out anyway.*
- *You just keep looking for faith! You may find it someday!* **Or...***Look how much faith you got! Now go and sit on your spiritual butt. Saved and waitin' for the grave.*

- *You can see the enemy picking and choosing a few folks out there, but you don't have any idea if you're part of the "in" crowd that's on their way to heaven. **Or...** The enemy loves everyone and no one is going to Hell.*
- *You blow it, yeah, but just believing in the Gospel is good enough. Grace is good and cheap.* **Or...** *You must do, do, do because you follow The Gospel plus Whatever-The-Church-Thinks-I-Should-Do-For-Salvation Plan.*

I love pushing people to either side. I can then plow doubt into those who believe, and plow disgust into those who get fed up.

There's lots of teachers out there who preach and teach this stuff. Lots of prideful folks grab that book and cherry-pick enough verses to support their position. They go to that book with their minds made up. They have no problem finding verses to support their ideas. They have to ignore the verses that don't fit; but that's OK. These people wow others with their charm and ear-ticklin' ideas. People will listen.

Baal-deCay once told us getting a person to go to one extreme or another will cause that person to go from **salvation to slavation** in no time. I dig that.

To: Wormwood <burnbabyburn@gothell.com>

From: Baal-Kobalt <capturetheplanet@brimstone.com>

Subject: Having an Edifice Complex

As we seek to undermine the churches, the very last statement in your list is quite potent. Let's call it "Religion versus. Relationship."

Human beings love belonging to something larger than themselves. We exploit that in the various Malevels, as you now well know. Churches are an especially rich environment for meeting this need. Humans want to feel pride in what they do and believe. They love to create an organization reflecting that sense of accomplishment.

They must, of course, have a big building to put it all in. They love to busy themselves like little manic bees. The building says, *Hey! Look at us… We are important! We are pious! We have the truth! Those folks meeting in that little shack down the street? Don't bother. Who would feel good about walking into that place? We are clearly blessed and those others guys? They're questionable in the faith department.*

In order to keep the organization running smoothly, humans create rules. That book provides some inspiration but the man-made ones are the most satisfying to human pride.

Oh, how these creatures love to create rules. The leaders love the control that their rules exert over their followers. These rules, which govern the followers' behavior will, if followed to the letter, show "true" piety to everyone in the organization. Following the rules becomes equivalent to being good. But the son pointed out to the Pharisees that while people appear very spiritual on the outside by following man-made rules (so respectable and neat) they are corrupt on the inside, filled with "dead man's bones."

The rules, the organization and the outward behavior all become more important than **an actual relationship with the enemy:** *I look good. I act good. I am good. Heaven is smiling on me because I follow the rules!*

Woe to anyone who tries to reform the organization! All organizations, because so much time, energy and money have been put into them, take on lives of their own.

Whatever the motives of the founders, whether sincere or evil, the organization will eventually become self-sustaining, with all the dutiful sheep doing what they are told, thinking they are pleasing the enemy. The truth is they are pleasing the people in the organization, getting approval, privileges and ego-strokes for all their supposed piety. The leaders love the control. They watch the sheep and make sure they are obedient by what they do. (Whether or not the leaders themselves are following the rules…well, rank has its privileges.)

In the end, those people who followed man-made rules, in man-made buildings, trying to fulfill man-made standards will someday get this rebuke from the son: "Not everyone who says to me, 'Lord, Lord,' will enter the kingdom of heaven, but only the one who does the will of my Father who is in heaven. Many will say to me on that day, 'Lord, Lord, did we not prophesy in your name and in your name drive out demons and in your name perform many miracles?' Then I will tell them plainly, 'I never knew you. Away from me, you evildoers!'"[36]

That rebuke will be music to the Dark Kingdom's ears.

Comments?

To: Baal-Kobalt <capturetheplanet@brimstone.com>

From: Wormwood <burnbabyburn@gothell.com>

Subject: Pride is as pride does

Hey BK! It's that Tower of Babel thing again!

Why did those folks want to build that tower? So they could "make a name for ourselves…"[37]

It's all about pride at the end of the day. Pride in what they believe, pride in their big building and pride that other people notice who they are.

I love it when man-made religion hooks up with pride. People get so tangled up in both that enemy fades out. I have noticed that humans say they love the enemy, but they are really gettin' hooked on such and such leader. The leader becomes the center of it all. The people are proud to go to Pastor So-and-so's church or they follow the teaching of Joe Pious Schmo and push money at him, defending him to the hilt.

Following the enemy's son? It's a lot harder to sit and listen to his voice. It's sooo much easier to turn on the TV, radio, computer or whatever and listen to another *person*. Religion can slowly hide the enemy from view. So can those leaders who claim to speak in his name.

Hey humans! Keep right on doin' that religion thing, 'cause some day the Dark Kingdom will provide you with the Ultimate Religion complete with the Ultimate Leader. You'll have lots of fancy buildings, tons of rules and a Man you can follow and admire.

You can stand back and watch those who won't follow our Man get what they deserve. Hell on earth? You betcha!

To: Wormwood <burnbabyburn@gothell.com>

From: Baal-Kobalt <capturetheplanet@brimstone.com>

Subject: Suffering--The Dark Lord's most potent weapon

Well said! Disrupting, damaging, damning…that is our endgame. If we can use religion to further this, we will.

Someday, followers of the son will justly deserve the Mark for wanting a relationship with the enemy over our Man of Action's religion. The Dark Lord rules over this planet and how often do these idiotic humans forget this?

The enemy's son, before he went to the cross, remarked, "Now is the time for judgment on this world; now the prince of this world will be driven out."[38]

Let talk about a personal favorite subject of mine, suffering. Whenever suffering occurs, we insinuate the enemy is to blame. This works for believers and non-believers. Even insurance companies have an "Acts of God" category.

The Dark Kingdom's role in suffering must be either downplayed or ruled out completely. We don't exist. If something goes wrong, humans will often take some level of responsibility (don't hold your breath on this) but if it's really big, they immediately question the enemy and his goodness. They will ignore the role that human choice plays and place the whole tragedy at the feet of the enemy.

The more you can encourage **completely** blaming the enemy, the better. Never cease to assassinate the enemy's character. Pester believers with *Why did this terrible thing happen?* Discourage people so they start talking less and less to the enemy. Emphasize the enemy's failures to act swiftly, thus encouraging them to start questioning who he is, in light of what little he does or doesn't do.

(This sets the stage for when the Man of Action shows up with solutions to all the world's problems. People will listen to him because he will promise to alleviate suffering and bring forth justice. We will insinuate this is something the enemy should have done, but didn't. But with our Man front and center, acting decisively and with results, the enemy will become irrelevant.)

Don't allow the idea to surface that suffering is sharing in the life of enemy's son. That annoying book makes it hard to keep the lies coming. Discourage people from believing this verse: "...because Christ also suffered for us, leaving us an example, that ye should follow his steps."[39]

No, no, no. We want the believer to ascribe malice or derelict of duty on the enemy's part and see what is happening as punishment or divine indifference. We never want the person to see it as chastening, which is correcting a person out of love. We find that just disgusting.

That baneful book says: "Endure hardship as discipline; God is treating you as his children...but God disciplines us for our good, in order that we may share in his holiness. No discipline seems pleasant at the time, but painful. Later on, however, it produces a harvest of righteousness and peace for those who have been trained by it."[40]

The goal of the enemy? Here it is: "Those whom I love I rebuke and discipline. So be earnest and repent."[41]

Suffering, as much as we detest this aspect of it, can bring a person closer to the enemy. The enemy seeks to mold his children's character, thereby gaining maturity. The enemy wants his children to serve him for who he is—not just for what he does for them. He wants them to trust him, for he always presents himself as trustworthy.

But we can pervert that: Harp on what he hasn't done, that his motives and character are suspect. Obedience to him will soon evaporate. Given enough time and disappointment, humans will take (to use your analogy) the steering wheel from the enemy and drive their own lives right off the cliff, much to our delight.

To: Baal-Kobalt <capturetheplanet@brimstone.com>
From: Wormwood <burnbabyburn@gothell.com>
Subject: Another spin

Hey BK! I agree that blaming the enemy for everything that goes wrong will cause people to be disgusted by him. I also think the opposite tactic is just as effective. The first tactic brings anger and disillusionment. Right on.

But this other tactic makes people fearful! So, let's hammer humans to stay focused **on just** the Dark Kingdom! *Help! Demons everywhere! They must be behind every illness, every disaster and everything that goes wrong!* If we keep harping on the Dark Kingdom's power and presence in this world, the kingdom of the enemy looks wimpier all the time.

Our rodeo needs to be so in your face that no one can ignore us. The enemy works behind the scenes, using love to get his followers to work in his kingdom. Yuck.

I love ginormous displays of evil: The Inquisition, slavery, 9/11, Auschwitz, Benghazi, Islamic State...these are just a few of my favorites. So, when people look at us with all our evil fireworks, the enemy looks puny. (We know better, but humans are so easily wowed by us). Hammer on about our power in this world and the Dark Kingdom will look bigger all the time. People will have a hard time seeing the good after a while.

Humans will see what we shove into their idiotic faces. They will forget the enemy's power. Our display of evil so rocks that humans get caught up in it. People have a whole industry built on showing the bad: "the nightly news." Good news? Nah. Journalists say, "If it bleeds, it leads." Happy to help. Humans make it so easy for us.

Enemy: small. The Dark Kingdom: ginormous. Score!

Some believers even see themselves as warriors against us, trying to bring down the Dark Kingdom by swinging their swords--that irritating book. They act in the enemy's name, of course, but soon they love being the center of attention: *Look at ME and my spiritual ability!* Their swords grow dull 'cause they're not sharpening them on the enemy's word.

Their focus is on themselves and that's a sure fire way to blunt the sword. The Dark Kingdom loves a dull sword. It may look good, but it doesn't pack a hack.

Without that book being front and center, believers fumble around like goofs and don't know the power they have in the son. I'll work to keep it that way.

> To: Wormwood <burnbabyburn@gothell.com>
>
> From: Baal-Kobalt <capturetheplanet@brimstone.com>
>
> Subject: How about this one?

Confusion is delightful: It keeps humans careening back and forth on waves of pride and doubt, power and fear, belief and disgust. Let's consider yet another approach.

We can so minimalize the Dark Kingdom's presence that any discussion about evil sounds positively medieval. Those who identify evil behavior in human beings with us will be seen as backwards and uninformed.

How then will society explain the behavior of its more recalcitrant members? Emphasize understanding human behavior by placing it into psychological and environmental categories only. Science coupled with compassion makes everyone feel so modern:

- *This person is not evil. Such an antiquated term. We must use compassionate terms.*
- *It was a bad childhood / abuse / racism / mental illness / society itself / homophobia, etc. that drove this poor individual to be who they are and do what they do.*

So, we can either stand brazenly in the spotlight, or we can stay hidden in the wings. Either way, we win.

We want people to be in bondage to anger and fear. They can either think we are all-powerful and the enemy is not, or they can think that evil really doesn't exist, so the problem of human behavior is solvable only with more research, diagnostics, compassion and medication.

The thought that the Dark Kingdom has the upper hand even makes the enemy's followers fearful. I have more than once sown doubt about this verse: "Ye are of God, little children, and have overcome them: because greater is he that is in you, than he that is in the world."[42]

When believers see how mightily our Lion roars, they cringe, losing sight of the enemy's promises. Redefining evil and searching for more scientific explanations for human behavior also makes believers uneasy.

Counselling, education and medications haven't been able to fix people. Explaining the behaviors of Jeffrey Dahmer, Ted Bundy or Charles Manson as simply coming from a bad childhood will leave people unsatisfied as to why humans do what they do. They secretly fear the next Charles Manson is growing up, because there is no shortage of abused and discarded children.

So, once again, the doubt we sow brings us a harvest of cowards and doubters. The ultimate harvest, my dreadful demon? People, especially believers, start to give up. In the face of such overwhelmingly powerful negative forces, hope lasts about as long as that snowball in Hell.

> To: Baal-Kobalt <capturetheplanet@brimstone.com>
> From: Wormwood <burnbabyburn@gothell.com>
> Subject: It all comes down to control

Hey BK! From what I've seen, humans hate to think the universe is random. Yeah, they like to blah-blah on about random blind forces evolving the whole creation into existence, but at a personal level, they fight back. They want to know why things go the way they do. If they are non-believers, they struggle to make sense of the chaos. If they are believers, they struggle to reconcile the enemy's promises with what they're seeing.

It just freezes my cheese that chaos can often get people to seek the enemy and his truth more deeply. It's way better when chaos gets people panicking, running away from the enemy and trying to fix it themselves. I dig that because they fall deeper into fear.

> To: Wormwood <burnbabyburn@gothell.com>
> From: Baal-Kobalt <capturetheplanet@brimstone.com>
> Subject: Keep all of this in mind!

Your point is well taken.

People will defend the position that the universe came from random forces as well as life itself. But, behind closed doors, the thought that their life has no purpose behind it, nor does the universe, makes them angry and afraid. People want life to have purpose and meaning.

Others are content to simply exist. They're akin to a soda can floating on the sea. They just bob up and down, taking no responsibility for their lives. They see no sense in exerting control, for they are sure that it will make no difference.

Either way, we win. Random forces and deep fatalism both undermine the supremacy of the enemy. Let's move on, shall we?

Our next tactic to render the church in the U.S. ineffective is to undermine the concept of sin itself. We need to repeatedly emphasize the view that human beings are, by nature, fundamentally **good.** By making aberrant behavior the result of environment or psychological conditions, humans will try to create the optimal environment and treatment. Every generation thinks they've found the real reasons for why people behave the way they do. They have discovered how to be better parents, how to create better schools, how to better solve poverty, and how to better treat social pathology than all the generations before them. Or, at least, that's what they tell themselves.

But, at the core of all this confidence, niggling doubts will surface. Despite all of the enlightened child-rearing techniques, the medications, and the good schooling, people still grow up and commit what the enemy calls sin: "For from the heart come evil thoughts, murder, adultery, all sexual immorality, theft, lying, and slander."[43]

Our Dark Lord calls this the "Your Children Are So Pathetic!" list and waves it whenever He can in the face of the enemy.

The churches now have even more niggling doubts. They preach forgiveness of sin, but sometimes wonder what sin really is. They approach that book's definitions with skepticism and worry. Their personal definitions, guided by an enlightened culture, don't quite match up with that book's. What that book calls "sin" gets transformed into "lifestyle."

Sin as sin got the full treatment on the cross. The enemy's son died for all sin. But today, some sins are not sins. The church has rearranged and re-categorized them in an effort to be more loving. The church is now loving people without emphasizing the process whereby they become more like the enemy's son.

The church is effectively handing many people a first-class ticket to Hell. I do not want to be there on that Day when the enemy asks his followers why they thought this sin or that sin was OK, despite what his book explicitly says.

Our tactic is evilly simple: Keep the focus away from Hell, sin and judgment (except for really bad people—Hitler, homophobes and the like) and pound the drumbeat of love, love, love. Make grace a very elastic concept: Forgiveness is easily given to a life carelessly led. Just focus on how the enemy's son loves everybody, no matter what. Deemphasize his stand on sin.

Can you give me an example of this application?

To: Baal-Kobalt <capturetheplanet@brimstone.com>

From: Wormwood <burnbabyburn@gothell.com>

Subject: On it!

Hey BK! The woman caught in the act of adultery is a good one. Hammer home only the part where the enemy's son told her that he forgave her. Downplay or even drop the "go and sin no more" part. Just pound home the message of love, love, love! No need to change your behavior, 'cause cheap grace is always right around the corner!

It all boils down to this: Believers feel self-righteous with their more compassionate view of the enemy. The old-school ways of doing church get thrown under the Let's-Be-A-Modern-Church Bus. That irritating book no longer enjoys center stage. It's largely gotten lost in the "Well, that's how you interpret it" debate or the "That's the way it was back then" debate.

"The Bible as the only foundation" gets really muddled in the modern church. Without that book being the only foundation, humans dream up all sorts of ideas and practices that do not square with the enemy's principles. These new ideas are not against that book, but they lessen the focus on it over time. That book seems less and less applicable. Less and less interesting. Less and less relevant. Then one day, the church is standing on its own power. Hey, humans are an energetic lot, and churches can keep going for a long time.

The enemy's presence disappears as churches seek his truth less and their own good feelings more. Without his power, lives don't changed. But everyone feels so good that they don't even notice he's outta there.

I love sheep who are weak, hopeless but baa-baa on about how relevant they are. I like to serve them, with mint jelly and a beer.

To: Wormwood <burnbabyburn@gothell.com>

From: Baal-Kobalt <capturetheplanet@brimstone.com>

Subject: You are certainly on point!

If people are not taught that they are sinners, and do not feel the weight of their sin, then the need for the power of the cross is not so apparent. The enemy's son paid the price to set people free from the power of sin and death.

The Dark Kingdom thrives on sin and death! We can ensnare humans all too easily with sin and death.

Churches, without the enemy's power infusing them, can then go several ways in their thinking:

- *Let's create an emphasis on feeling good, prosperous and happy. If people feel good, then they think they are good. Good thoughts lead to good behavior, right?*
- *Let's focus more on a cause than debating about theology. Energy for the enemy should go into working on social issues and fervor for him should go into the cause. People don't mean to relegate the enemy into the background, but that's what eventually happens.*
- *Let's foster experience-centered faith. People don't necessarily need theological teaching and personal discipline. Eventually, life's hard experiences and unanswered questions will become more challenging to a faith that largely emotional.*
- *Let's emphasize that the sin nature is gone forever and focus only on the "new man." Let's teach that sin is "all in the past." We will encourage our people with "you must have more faith!" (Some, of course, will privately feel they can never get ahead of the sin curve, but won't admit this.) People will feel spiritually superior to others with all of the faith they profess. They won't confess any negative thoughts or struggles, fearful of hindering their faith. People feel in control with their faith. One way to show how much faith they have is to put money into the very ministries who teach this.*

When the old sin nature rears up its ugly head time and time again, we enjoy watching all hell break loose in the souls of such people. Such people will share with others how faith-filled they are to overcompensate for the deep fear and failure they feel inside.

Let's review that last one for a moment. Boiling down christianity to a simple altar call and then asserting that a new believer is now instantaneously changed, ignores an uncomfortable truth: the old sin nature is still there.

Yes, the new nature is now present, but the old nature now wants to kill the new baby nature. We can always exploit this old nature and make the new believer wonder what's going wrong. A new believer now faces a conundrum:

- *Why do I keep sinning?*
- *Why am I tempted all the time?*
- *Why can't I overcome _____? (Fill in the sin)*

If we emphasize **experience in lieu of a lifetime process of walking in the transformative power of the enemy's spirit,** then we can undermine the new believer's faith. We can even derail it altogether, given enough pounding. Following the enemy's son is a journey, not a quick trip through a spiritual car wash.

Get churches to encourage this by only quoting those verses about old things passing away and the new coming—avoid the verses about walking in the enemy's spirit and transformation by the renewing of the mind. Focus on Paul's accomplishments, not his struggles. That way, this "new creation" thing implies immediate victory over sin—not a lifetime of discipline and staying in step with the enemy's spirit.

Remember how we talked about the power the son gives his followers to lead the life he calls them to? Downplay the relationship aspect. Focus just on the struggle with sin and how long it is lasting. Don't let new believers spend too much time with the enemy, so they can't learn the enemy's voice. We must promote the idea that walking with the enemy is **not** a struggle. It's a piece of cake.

Whisper that if someone is struggling:

- *Maybe you were born that way.*
- *Maybe you're not really saved.*
- *You must have more faith (faith is a gift from the enemy as well, but distract them from that with their supposed inadequacy).*
- *Maybe this born-again idea is overrated.*
- *Maybe this whole born-again thing is a lie.*

Yes, I know, the enemy has delivered many people from dreadful habits, but the sin nature is still there. People want to avoid the heavy lifting that discipline implies. They want a quick fix to who they are and what they've done.

Paul saw that the only hope for him to overcome his sin nature was through the enemy's son. That took time and a commitment to the process.

For Hell's sake, don't let the believer stand on the revelation that Paul had about his deliverance in the son; focus the believer's attention on how often the battle is lost and how sin is way too powerful to overcome. Or, maybe it is not even sin—it is just who you are.

I am so sorry we lost Paul. He was a major asset before he was knocked off his donkey and then became one himself.

To: Baal-Kobalt <capturetheplanet@brimstone.com>

From: Wormwood <burnbabyburn@gothell.com>

Subject: Still bugged by that "new creation" idea

Hey BK! Creating something new takes time. If our idiot humans took that blasted book seriously, they'd see how even the enemy took time to make order out of chaos, when he created the universe and everything in it.

How can believers think anything different? Just add the boiling water of faith to Insta-christian and away we go? Forgiveness? Yeah, that's given in an instant. Entrance into the enemy's Kingdom? Yes: that's instant as well.

Becoming like the enemy's son? That takes time. But in this modern microwave world, people want a deep faith in 30 seconds. I tell 'em, *you keep on thinking that.*

To: Wormwood <burnbabyburn@gothell.com>

From: Baal-Kobalt <capturetheplanet@brimstone.com>

Subject: Who's to blame? The list is endless!

Humans are so impatient. They want the quick route to glory.

If the sin nature is downplayed or thought to be utterly gone with a one-time simple confession of faith, humans must come up with another reason for why they can't seem to walk consistently in the faith. We know that the old nature is a mine field for blowing up the confidence that a believer has in the enemy.

Redirect the believer to consider joining the BLAME GAME. Blame is a beautiful thing—it takes away all personal responsibility and lays failure at the feet of others.

A person, instead of becoming a disciple and focusing on following the enemy wholeheartedly day by day, will instead focus on those people and situations that have caused hurt and disappointment, and thus must be causing a believer's failure to thrive.

How do you get a plant to thrive? Put it in the sun. Water it. Feed it. So obvious, yet those who follow the enemy easily forget this simple truth. The greatest way for someone to become more like the son is to spend time in his presence. Believers should listen to him. (I think otherwise, of course.)

The son uses that book to water and feed the believer's heart. He calls to the believer's heart—deep calling to deep. But in this Gotta-Go-Gotta-Do world, hearing the shepherd's voice is becoming more and more challenging.

Soon, the son's voice is lost to negative experiences and the never-ending drumbeat of "The World Is Going to Hell in a Handbasket." That's exactly what we want that person to hear. All the time.

People today like the word "survivor." Good. That pesky book instead says that those who follow the enemy are "more than conquerors." Not good. Victims, not victors, is what we are striving for in the Dark Kingdom.

To: Baal-Kobalt <capturetheplanet@brimstone.com>

From: Wormwood <burnbabyburn@gothell.com>

Subject: Why not forgive AND forget sin?

Hey BK! Why does the enemy forgive his followers' sin but won't let them forget? Of course, always parading a person's sin in front of their shocked faces is a personal pastime of mine. What's the enemy's strategy here?

To: Wormwood <burnbabyburn@gothell.com>

From: Baal-Kobalt <capturetheplanet@brimstone.com>

Subject: Rain fire on their parade!

It is true that the enemy promises to cleanse their hearts from sin's stain. That loser John (exiling him to that island was not harsh enough) writes: "If we confess our sins, he is faithful and just to forgive us our sins, and to cleanse us from all unrighteousness."[44]

New believers will embrace the forgiveness the enemy offers for a while…until we get to them. Parading their sins before them is such a delight. The cross then fades from view and their transgressions grow larger and larger, soon crowding out the cross altogether.

As a tactic to undermine faith, this is so easily accomplished. Humans are never short of sin-fries in their little unhappy meals, and the more we can exploit this, the more they doubt their salvation. Suggestions?

To: Baal-Kobalt <capturetheplanet@brimstone.com>

From: Wormwood <burnbabyburn@gothell.com>

Subject: Just crank up the heat

Hey BK! The enemy forgives his children so he can hang out with them. He hates being apart from them, but there's a catch: he can't look at their sin-filled souls. He won't force himself into their lives without them inviting him in.

I suppose that's what love is all about. There's gotta be a choice. The enemy won't invade his children's space. He set it up that way from the beginning. I was taught that after he made this planet and planted that Garden, he hung out there.

Why? Dunno.

The Dark Lord loves force. It's a lot more fun.

The enemy waits for his children to ask him to forgive their sin. He already knows about it, but wants them to cop to it. That's what confession is. A believer agrees with the enemy that they've sinned. Well, duh. To be human is to be knee-deep in the alligator sin-swamp.

Why all this "Forgive me! I've sinned!" business and the enemy bending over backwards to do so is way beyond me. The enemy hung out with Adam and Eve. He still wants to hang out with those maggots' children.

I love running the movie, "This Is Your Sin, Loser" in someone's head. Daily, if I can. I'm guessing that the enemy forgives the sin yet lets them remember it to keep them humble. Humans are more compassionate if they can remember having been in that set of shoes. I guess it's hard to be a self-righteousness-stick-in-the-holy-mud if you can remember sin and how it felt, but also remember forgiveness and how it felt.

Our Dark Lord be praised! Sin and human nature go together like horse poop and flies. They give us lots of ammo to shoot at humans. I love it when believers can't think or act because of all that fear and shame! A stuck believer serves the Dark Kingdom well. If a believer ain't serving the kingdom of the enemy, they're servin' us.

The enemy's son said that a follower is either for him or for us. He was teaching those dim-wits about taking away the property (the enemy's children) of the "strong man." (Who'd want 'em?) While the Dark Lord didn't like the enemy's son's teaching, I bet He sure dug that title. I sure did.

To: Wormwood <burnbabyburn@gothell.com>

From: Baal-Kobalt <capturetheplanet@brimstone.com>

Subject: Sin is the gift that keeps on giving

I applaud your observations.

The enemy wants to forgive. That we certainly know. He equally seeks repentance from his children. Repentance is changing direction. We covered that: It is a holy U-turn, if you will, on the part of a human who wants to walk in that forgiveness.

But, as I said, we can cheapen grace by emphasizing it over and over, and downplay actually changing the behavior and attitude that put the person in trouble in the first place...Sin. Grace. Sin. Grace. Sin. Grace, etc. Monotonous, certainly, but this drum-beat over time become the numb-beat of a person's walk.

Humans have one trait we capitalize on all the time: The more they use something, the less valuable it becomes. They become used to it, and it loses its special quality. Grace, used over and over, will lose its power in a person's life. The cross becomes ho-hum. The enemy becomes hum-drum. The person becomes spiritually dum-dum. We rejoice.

I have a few more ideas to share with you on how to render the church useless. Remember how susceptible Eve was to any suggestions about that fruit? Forbidden fruit is the juiciest! So, dangle sexual temptation in front of believers' quivering nostrils whenever you can. With the proliferation of porn—the Dark Lord be praised—this is getting easier and easier all the time. Sex is one of the enemy's kindest gifts to humankind.

So, the Dark Lord drew a target on it as soon as He could. The beauty of sexual degradation is you can bring down the young, the old, the believer and the non-believer. Sexual sin is the one appetite that a human cannot satisfy. If anything, their "taste-buds" get blunted and they crave more and more.

If you keep this temptation constantly knocking at the door, some believers will grow tired of being good and succumb to thinking:

- *Hey, I deserve this!*
- *I have been good…a little time with sin won't hurt.*
- *Besides, I can handle it!*
- *And even if I can't, forgiveness is always just around the corner…*

Downplay how sin can entangle someone. A little sin here, a little sin there. Delude believers into thinking they can walk away anytime from whatever they are dabbling in. All the while, we are pulling the noose even tighter.

Now, believers might think: *How will this behavior look to others?* If that crosses their minds, I suggest you remind them of the people in church who are doing the same thing or **worse.** Put the sin into perspective: *You are not so bad. At least you didn't do **that.***

Believers might think: *I am not hurting anyone with my sin! It's my own private happy place.* Yes. Keep fanning the flames of that delusion. It's like the guy who decided to drill a hole under his seat in a full lifeboat. Everyone got mad as they saw him starting to drill. His response? "Hey, it's only under my seat!"

Believers might think: *How unfair to call who I am sinful! I am sincere.* Yes, you are, my gullible human. But, you can be sincerely wrong. That's why, if we minimize the standards of that dreadful book, then sincerity replaces sin.

Here's a good one. Believers might think: *It's all culturally determined anyway. Moral absolutes are so old-school; we need to be creative in this complicated world.* What was sinful then needs a more enlightened approach now. We don't kill witches anymore, now do we? Keep this one on the table.

If you can reduce that book down to mere cultural prohibitions, then its principles, which transcend culture, can be marginalized. The less that book calls the shots, the more the culture will, as we have discussed.

The enemy's son died for all sin and to him it is all despicable. We know that it impairs the enemy's contact with his children. Even the enemy's son cried about being forsaken as he bore the weight of all of the world's sin on his dying shoulders. I despise that the enemy's son wants his followers to possess attitudes and behaviors reflective of his life in them. He wants to see fruit.

We like fruit too: The kind that once you take a bite, its poison slowly but surely deadens the soul.

To: Baal-Kobalt <capturetheplanet@brimstone.com>

From: Wormwood <burnbabyburn@gothell.com>

Subject: Yeah! Bring on the tsunami of sin!

Hey BK! I find that rolling small waves of temptation towards new believers where they can gingerly hop over them is a good way to persuade them of their new-found power over sin. They grow increasingly confident that they have truly changed. They play along sin's shore with their "I'm a New Creation" Boogie Board.

I then love to sit up on the cliffs, watching the tsunami of sin slam into them…Bye-bye! Being swept away by the very thing they thought they could control is a cool way to shake up faith. Added bonus: they shake the faith of others too!

> To: Wormwood <burnbabyburn@gothell.com>
> From: Baal-Kobalt <capturetheplanet@brimstone.com>
> Subject: Relevant? Pshaw!

I picture the Beached Boys, singing in Hawaiian shirts and as their melodies drift across the sea, another naïve Christian sinks heavily to the sea floor, where he or she joins the many skeletons scattered about.

The Dark Kingdom, like a Great White, prowls around for any signs of life. If a whiff of hope remains, our jaws are open wide, ready to devour. We still have a few more tactics to review for undermining the church.

Emphasize repeatedly the question: How could God be relevant to our modern age? How could a Jewish teacher, who lived 2,000 years ago, be of any interest to today? So, when a modern person asks, "Where can I go for answers to all those nagging questions?"

We shout, "Step right up!" We offer:

- The Big Bang to answer the "How did the universe get here?" question
- Mr. C. Darwin to answer the "How did humans get here?" question
- Psychology to answer the "Why do we do what we do?" question
- Medication to answer the "How can I feel better?" question
- Political activism to answer the "How can I change things?" question
- Spirituality to answer the "How can I avoid organized religion?" question
- Academia to answer the "What do I need to know?" question

- Popular culture to answer the "What's interesting?" question
- News media to answer the "What's important?" question
- Activism to answer the "What can I pour all my worship into?" question
- Social media to answer the "Who am I?" question
- The latest public opinion poll to answer the "What is right and wrong?" question

No need anymore for the enemy's answers to any of life's important questions. Numb and dumb: That's how we want people to be. Encourage people to hanker after lots of distractions, with video games, technology, social media and reality TV leading the way.

The enemy's message will be overrun by the cultural horde of distractions. If people go to church, (much to our regret) they are there maybe two hours a week. That leaves us plenty of time during the rest of the week to undo those two hours. Keep people focused on inconsequential matters or give them easy answers that don't require much thought. With just enough knowledge in their possession, self-righteousness and fanatical certainty will fill in the gaps.

Numb and dumb, my demon: that is our sole/soul goal.

Even the enemy uses the idea of sheep to designate his followers. He's their shepherd and he watches over them, and warns them of wolves. (We take that as a compliment)

But, if we can encourage the sheep to be numb and dumb, with distractions drowning out the shepherd's voice, then dinner is served.

> To: Baal-Kobalt <capturetheplanet@brimstone.com>
> From: Wormwood <burnbabyburn@gothell.com>
> Subject: Where we DON'T want them to go for answers

Hey BK! Love it. Here's my list.

A truly modern person says, "At least I know where I **don't** want to go for answers!" *Good for you, you modern-thinking person. We support you **not** looking into:*

- Christianity: It has supported all sorts of bigotry and abuse and is narrow-minded and judgmental
- Parents: What do they know?
- Conservatives of Any Stripe: What good is the past? Only now matters
- Anything Outside MY Generation: We know what we know—good enough
- History: Boring
- Books: Boring—two-second sound bites and You Tube are good enough
- Experts: Who can you trust? Go to your friends—your peer group is more in touch with what you are going through than anyone else
- Bible: Culturally insensitive and increasingly irrelevant
- Family: Nah--with Mom's boyfriends moving in and out all the time, and Dad's not around, family becomes those people I choose to love
- Religion: It's so hypocritical--it's caused more deaths in history than anything else

Yeah, I know: More people died in the 20th century because of leaders who took the enemy's role in people's hearts and then demanded their followers do terrible things in the name of the State. A heck of a lot more bodies piled up in recent history than all those wars of religion put together. If young people don't know history, don't talk to older folks who went through difficult times and only listen to their peers, then we can keep the sheep numb and dumb.

The tactics you've given me are right on. Some I've done and others I will do! I will work quickly because some of the enemy's followers get our agenda. They are praying, studying that book and have a no-compromise attitude with the culture. They may be small, but they are mighty.

It's that David and Goliath thing all over again. I'd like the giant to win this time.

To: Wormwood <burnbabyburn@gothell.com>

From: Baal-Kobalt <capturetheplanet@brimstone.com>

Subject: Battleground? No, a playground!

Remember the context of that David-Goliath encounter? It was a war. We are still in a war. You know that. I know that. The Dark Kingdom knows that.

The followers of the enemy's son? Some understand this reality and some do not.

When Adam and Eve were driven out of the Eden, they should have gone from being gardeners to guerillas. Instead, they became goofs. They were shocked and amazed when Cain murdered Abel. What were they expecting? With sin's poison seeping into every pore of creation, what was Cain supposed to do? "Group hug, everyone!" I think not.

Every generation has its exceptions to this blindness, however. A.W. Tozer was one of those followers who seemed to understand fully what this engagement between the two kingdoms entailed. I quote him at length because it is people who think like him that must silenced in the coming days. He observed that America's very foundation was laid on such an understanding of this war:

"In the early days, when Christianity exercised a dominant influence over American thinking, men conceived the world to be a battleground. Our fathers believed in sin and the devil and hell as constituting one force, and they believed in God and righteousness and heaven as the other. By their very nature, these forces were opposed to each other forever in deep, grave, irreconcilable hostility. Man…had to choose sides…and if he choose to come out on God's side, he could expect open war with God's enemies. The fight would be real and deadly and would last as long as life continued here below. Men looked forward to heaven as a return from the wars…to enjoy in peace the home prepared for them."[45]

Such perception, my dark demon, must be replaced with deception. We certainly can't have such dangerous ideas like these being brought forth from the pulpit. It is teachings such as these that need to be buried under the scrap heap of history, not just thrown on top. That is why what you do is so necessary in the days to come.

Mr. Tozer readily admits that:

"How different today…Men think of the world not as a battleground, but as a playground. We are not here to fight; we are here to frolic. We are not in a foreign land; we are at home. We are not getting ready to live, but we are already living, and the best we can do is rid ourselves of our inhibitions and our frustrations and live this life to the full. This…is the religious philosophy of modern man…"[46]

Here, in essence, is what we must downplay to the fullest: The followers of the son cannot be soldiers—they must be sybarites. Do you know what a sybarite is? It is a person who engages in luxuries, hedonism and just plain living life "to the full."

You are needed to be actively engaged in helping followers hand in their shields and beat their swords into lawn chairs.

> To: Baal-Kobalt <capturetheplanet@brimstone.com>
> From: Wormwood <burnbabyburn@gothell.com>
> Subject: From Armor to "Amour"

Hey BK! I am stoked I am a part of this! I know that blow-hard book goes on and on about putting on the "full armor of God."[47]

But if we downplay the "battleground" bit and play up the "playground" bit, that armor talk seems to out-of-date and just plain boring. I think we should replace the "armor of God" with the "amour" for the world!

> To: Wormwood <burnbabyburn@gothell.com>
> From: Baal-Kobalt <capturetheplanet@brimstone.com>
> Subject: Change of clothes—no fun intended

Of course, that baneful book equates following the son with warfare—we know there's a war going on; the son knows it; but do his followers really know just how serious this war is? So, to further attack the church, may I suggest some replacements for each piece of the armor?

I must again quote Paul, much to my disgust. Let's break down that armor and all its parts so we claim them for our own:

"Therefore put on the full armor of God, so that when the day of evil comes, you may be able to stand your ground, and after you have done everything, to stand."[48]

*But the armor of the world is so easy to put on! When evil shows up, stand on **our** ground, and after you have done everything to **compromise, blend in.** No worries! The world won't even notice you. It will leave you alone. The son talked about his followers facing persecution. With our armor on, that will not be an issue.*

"Stand firm then, with the belt of truth buckled around your waist…"[49]

Wear an elastic band that flexes with your moves and your ways. Truth should be elastic, adaptable to ever-changing situations and always compatible with the changes in the world.

"The breastplate of righteousness in place…"[50]

No. Have an open mind and open heart instead. Embrace everyone and don't judge. Protecting your heart implies we have bad things in store for you. No. We want your heart filled with love…love that floats and flits and never takes a stand. We want welfare not warfare in your heart, you silly follower.

"Your feet fitted with the readiness that comes from the gospel of peace…"[51]

Why be ready? Ready for what? To run in with your truth and deny others the right to walk in their own? The "gospel of peace"—really now. It is more like the Gospel of Malice. Don't try to convert others. That is not peace. If the shoe fits, throw it out.

"In addition to all this, take up the shield of faith, with which you can extinguish all the flaming arrows of the evil one."[52]

You don't need a shield! What lies! You need an embrace from the One we serve. Open your arms to everyone! Those aren't flaming arrows! Those are guiding lights, lighting the way to a more thoughtful, generous world. Doesn't everyone want one world, filled with love and belief in the goodness of Man? Let's have a group hug and look to the future. Let's just keep loving the planet.

"Take the helmet of salvation..."[53]

No. Minds should be like parachutes...better when open. Keep your mind free to listen to the wisdom that the enemy doesn't want you to have. This piece of armor implies you will receive blows from us. No. You will receive knowledge, revelation and a better way to go than anything the enemy has to offer.

"The sword of the Spirit, which is the word of God..."[54]

That book needs to burn. It has caused more strife than any other book around. You don't need a sword—you need a candle. Light up the darkness with your candle of good thoughts and sincere actions. That book causes division. We bring unity. Whatever you believe to be good, then it is so. You, as a truly modern person, will walk down the world's runway, light on your feet, open to all wisdom and championing the planet. We are not evil; christianity is.

"And pray in the Spirit on all occasions with all kinds of prayers and requests. With this in mind, be alert and always keep on praying for all the Lord's people."[55]

You, a fully modern person, may want to reconsider following the son. If you do pray, let it be, "Save me from the Lord's people."

> To: Baal-Kobalt <capturetheplanet@brimstone.com>
> From: Wormwood <burnbabyburn@gothell.com>
> Subject: Project Runaway

Hey BK! I dig your make-over! No more war, just a wardrobe. No more battles, just baubles. No more discernment, just adornment. Love it. This "armor of God" business is to remind the son's follower that they're in a war and they need to be ready, willing and able to take orders from the enemy. Don't you find it kinda weird that the Dark Kingdom's army is always ready, willing and able to raise Hell when called to do so?

Look at that belt of truth part: The truth holds everything up. Without truth, a soldier can't run without tripping. That blowhard book says, "…let us throw off everything that hinders and the sin that so easily entangles. And let us run with perseverance the race marked out for us, fixing our eyes on Jesus, the pioneer and perfecter of faith."[56]

That bombastic Paul tells Timothy: "No soldier in active service entangles himself in the affairs of everyday life, so that he may please the one who enlisted him as a soldier."[57]

A tightly buckled truth, based on the enemy's son who called himself "The Way, the Truth and the Life," helps the soldier to stand, waiting for his orders.

I'm gonna do all I can to trip such a soldier up.

On to the next bit: that breastplate. Ya gotta protect the heart and lungs. How human body works is a mystery to me, but I remember something about the heart pumps the blood through the body. But the blood is only as good as the oxygen it carries. It receives the oxygen from the lungs.

Lungs get it from the air, so the lungs connect the inside to the outside.

The soldier must protect what keeps him going. Spiritually, it's no different. The heart hears the orders and the lungs fill with breath of the enemy's life. The soldier is now ready to fight. He may be earth-bound, but his "lungs" join his earthly life to his heavenly calling. Righteousness is the strongest stuff to wear. The son provides the righteousness, making the soldier's heart ready. The soldier gets power from the son's own breath. I'm gonna keep my eye on such a soldier.

That fitted feet business: Tight, well-fitted shoes are what a soldier needs. The son is fitted onto the soldier's heart and mind. This soldier then can march strong in the enemy's might. The marching has one goal: to bring hope to the hopeless and provide peace to the chaos.

I'm gonna march with a more enticing beat.

That faith shield and putting out the darts bit: The soldier outfits his body for war. The soldier's body being protected ain't enough, 'cause we love to send flaming arrows right at the soldier. Up goes the shield of faith. Even when the volley is so dense it blocks out the son, the soldier holding up the shield of faith shows his confidence in the enemy's word.

I'm gonna make such a soldier wish he or she had stayed home.

OK, now on to that helmet: Yup, you gotta protect the head. It is a battleground, and needs protection from our pounding. That helmet stops the soldier from hitting the dirt. The soldier with those armor pieces is able to protect himself.

I'm gonna get that soldier to doubt that helmet. While he or she has taken it off to look at it because I've thrown in itchy doubt, down comes my sword.

That sword being the enemy's word bit: This is the one piece the soldier uses to defend himself. A soldier who knows it by heart and trains by it will be pretty dang scary on the battlefield. That book teaches all about the battle, the battle plan, the tactics, and the outcome. Such intel used by a strong soldier will give enemy's Kingdom victories. If that intel sits on a shelf, getting all dusty, then the soldier goes out guided by feelings and little bit of belief. I then can say, "Bye-bye soldier."

What bugs me is how it's the spirit's sword. The enemy is holding it right along with the soldier. A soldier in the enemy's army doesn't ever fight alone. That soldier is good to go and the son fights right along with him.

But hey, we fight right along with those deceived folks who are in the Dark Kingdom's army, too!

To: Wormwood <burnbabyburn@gothell.com>

From: Baal-Kobalt <capturetheplanet@brimstone.com>

Subject: March on

This is why we are training our soldiers with such urgency. We want to create as much havoc and destruction as we can before the son's forces rally. We will likewise equip and accompany our soldiers into each battle. The enemy claims we counterfeit everything that he does. But I say we are The Truth, the Real Deal, and he counterfeits **us**. Regardless, we will do everything in our dark power to decimate the enemy's forces. That is why you and I are working as hard as we are.

Your review of the tactics of how to derail the christian church in the U.S. is now complete. We will send you updates as we go.

Our next stop is how to destroy marriage and the family in the U.S. We don't have to work too hard on this one—these humans are doing a fine job.

To: Baal-Kobalt <capturetheplanet@brimstone.com>

From: Wormwood <burnbabyburn@gothell.com>

Subject: Wow!

Hey BK! You know that bombastic book better than most of the enemy's followers. You understand its teachings and see through its nonsense.

I guess you gotta know something well enough to twist it cleverly to confuse someone, right?

To: Wormwood <burnbabyburn@gothell.com>

From: Baal-Kobalt <capturetheplanet@brimstone.com>

Subject: 10% Truth + 90% Lie = 100% Effective

To quote that dastardly A. W. Tozer again: "The devil is a better theologian than any of us and is a devil still."

He, of course, was being dismissive. We take his words as a compliment.

I will be in touch very soon with your next aspect of training.

Stay in touch and stay in trouble.

NSA Release No. 3

Contents:
- Emails Regarding The Second Target: Marriage and the Family in the U.S.

> To: Wormwood <burnbabyburn@gothell.com>
> From: Baal-Kobalt <capturetheplanet@brimstone.com>
> Subject: Away we go!

Welcome to the final stage of your training to undermine the U.S. and render it an irrelevant and irreverent nation.

We now focus on destroying marriage and the family.

The enemy made a grave (pun intended) mistake when he compared marriage to his relationship to his children. He wanted to show his love and desire for spiritual intimacy by equating his relationship to his children in terms they could understand. Back in the day, if his children worshipped other gods, the enemy played the adultery card, right along with the jealousy card.

Why he cares so much for these maggots is beyond comprehension. Here are a few of the more nauseating passages:

- "For thy Maker is thine husband; the Lord of hosts is his name…" [58]
- "And he saith unto me, Write, Blessed are they which are called unto the marriage supper of the Lamb…"[59]
- "And I will betroth thee unto me forever; yea, I will betroth thee unto me in righteousness, and in judgment, and in lovingkindness, and in mercies. I will even betroth thee unto me in faithfulness: and thou shalt know the Lord."[60]
- "When Israel was a child, then I loved him, and called my son out of Egypt."[61]

The enemy even made Hosea marry a prostitute to show how Israel had committed adultery by chasing after other gods.

The enemy wanted to demonstrate through Hosea and his wayward wife that their marriage now reflected Israel's relationship to him.

See my point, my wily Wormwood? Because the enemy uses marriage, a tender father and family bonds to illustrate who he is, we must twist and ultimately destroy these comparisons. We thus engage in one of the most beneficial activities on the Dark Kingdom's behalf: **assassinating the enemy's character.**

Humans are plunging marriage and family into more and more chaos. We can now associate the enemy's character with that chaos. This is our goal. Period.

The Western World seems eager to destroy the very foundation that the enemy laid out in that Garden so long ago. We're already helping the destruction along, and greatly desire to accelerate it, per the wishes of our Dark Lord.

If we leave these positive associations with marriage, family and fathers alone, then the enemy can continue to use them for his purposes. But if we assault marriage, family and fathers, the enemy's character is called into question. We are seeking to render him extinct in the lives of his children. Think how wretched he will be thought of if the word "father" is considered a negative term.

Or better yet…who needs a father/Father at all?

> To: Baal-Kobalt <capturetheplanet@brimstone.com>
> From: Wormwood <burnbabyburn@gothell.com>
> Subject: Slappin' folks with the cold mackerel of reality

Hey BK! I dig your idea of making marriage, father and family so ugly that when the enemy uses those words to describe himself, people will run from him faster than a nudist in an ice storm.

The enemy's values are just plain laughable today. People just can't do what he demands. I'll harp on just how out of touch he is with his creation. My message is:

- *Do it yourself.*
- *Be yourself.*
- *Follow yourself.*

These stupid creatures are doing their own thing; they're thumbing their noses at the enemy and his word. They're tryin' to reinvent the morality wheel. But, yup, their lives then go bad. Real bad.

The cold mackerel of reality slaps them upside the head, because the enemy's word (I hate to admit this) is the best path for these idiot children to follow. Yessiree, it's that blame thing again! When humans ignore the enemy's will for their lives, doin' it their way, their lives crash and burn. But who's to blame? Not them, oh no never. It's the enemy! Ignore him then blame him. Sweet.

I love droppin' reality bombs on the enemy's ideas about marriage and family:

- **Sex should be kept within marriage.** Yup. Sure. Snicker. With all of the sexual temptation today (thank you, Internet!) and no real consequences (thank you antibiotics and abortion clinics!) why not go for it? Friends with benefits, hook-ups, one night stands, 'til love do us part: sex is nothing special. *Forget the spiritual oneness thing. It's just another appetite that needs filling. It's recreation. No big deal.*

- **Marriage is a spiritual union.** Blah. That blasted book says the enemy created humans as male and female. Marriage shows that unity. Yeah, right. Love's the only reason to get together. Old-school views on gender and biology need to be thrown out the window. *Human sexuality is whatever you want it to be. Who you are and what you do is your choice! That stupid male/female thing needs to be kicked to the curb. Create an identity! Follow your bliss!*

- **Marriage reflects Christian values.** Yup. Wait till that narcissism creeps in and marriage's only purpose is to make YOU happy, happy, happy! Go to church and forgive one another until it's your spouse—then WHAM! Go to court and let 'em have it. *Of course, God wants you to be happy...What? That's not happening? Get a divorce. God will forgive you. Oh, the second marriage didn't work out? That's OK! Then get a divorce. God will forgive you. It's better for the children, right? They can watch love and forgiveness at church and read about it in that book. Modeled at home? Nah.*

- **The family was created in the Garden of Eden.** Sure. Right. Families are divided, derided and constantly being re-decided. If two people love each other—well, that's good enough to get a family started. If a single person wants a baby, why not? *Love alone is enough to raise a child. Be more inclusive! Let the modern family and marriage become the way things are! Love is all you need!*

- **Fathers are important in a child's life.** This ain't the 1950's, baby. "Honey, I'm home!" is only on TV. Have you seen today's fathers? Many women call them "sperm donors" and that's all they're good for. They groove on and then move on. If Daddy happens to be around, he seems to be more involved with work and his life than his kids. *Hey, Dad! Your kids have* *their tablets, their phones and the Internet. You have yours. You're good to go.*

- **Mothers are important in a child's life.** Well, the culture hasn't totally pushed moms aside, but just like the men, moms' careers are more important than the kids. Forty hours in day care? No problem! Kids do better if they are socialized, right? I know that tired moms are less involved. Less from them means more input from us. *No worries! The culture will raise your kids, Mom.*

I love showin' just how outta touch the enemy is. Love then morphs into an idol: Folks believe it will make everything good. Uh-huh. Sure.

To: Wormwood <burnbabyburn@gothell.com>

From: Baal-Kobalt <capturetheplanet@brimstone.com>

Subject: Love, love, love

When love as the only basis for marriage--*Why shouldn't two people who love each other get married?*--collides with narcissistic humans expecting personal happiness to be the highest goal--*I deserve to be happy!*—then watch the fires burn.

Love is an odd thing, really. It cannot flourish when selfishness is in the soil. That blasted book even outlines real love in the 13th chapter of Corinthians. We hate that chapter. I am glad it's only read at weddings.

Humans are so prone to forget the enemy's words once the honeymoon is over. You do not see couples reading that passage on their anniversaries, do you?

Marriage is well on its way to becoming such a ridiculous institution that it has to be reinvented. Humans, having made such a mess of it, figure if they reinvent it, they'll get it right in its new forms. Ah, yes. You just keep thinking that, my deluded humans.

To: Baal-Kobalt <capturetheplanet@brimstone.com>

From: Wormwood <burnbabyburn@gothell.com>

Subject: R.I.P.

Hey BK! Sexual pleasure and narcissism are perfect bedfellows. (Yup: pun intended!) You can just hear what those moderns are thinkin':

- *It's all about ME! It's all about my needs and wants.*
- *Porn, sexually explicit movies, sex as recreation, adultery--all become ways for ME to find fulfillment.*
- *I am not hurting anyone with my sin.*
- *Even if I do, they'll get over it.*
- *I am entitled to feel good.*
- *A little sin in my head is not the real thing. So, it's not really sin, is it?*

People don't get married anymore just because they've had sex. Doctors clear up STDs and the state can take care of children who slip pass the abortion clinic. Multiple dads, deadbeat dads, no dads: Don't be responsible, men. Split. So what if your kids enter a world with little or no security? Even birds build nests and protect their young. You men? Not so much. Happy to help ya!

To: Wormwood <burnbabyburn@gothell.com>

From: Baal-Kobalt <capturetheplanet@brimstone.com>

Subject: May I take your dis-order, please?

Good! If "love" is the answer, then make "What's in it for me?" the question.

Here's another tactic for undermining marriage and the family: Pervert love, and make it lust. Lust is an appetite that no matter how many times humans sit at the table, they still want more, more, more. Sexual temptations, coupled with disrespect for marriage, will create chaos. That is our business, my demon: chaos.

The enemy brought order to chaos. We have been trying to undo it ever since. That baneful book says, "In the beginning God created the heaven and the earth. And the earth was without form, and void; and darkness was upon the face of the deep."[62]

The enemy spoke, and we rue the day he brought light out of darkness, order out of disarray, and life out of stillness. But, in their willingness to listen to the Dark Lord, those First Parents opened a gate for us to enter in.

We gladly reintroduced chaos back into creation, especially in the lives of the enemy's children. Each element the enemy imposed on humans for order becomes, in our hands, **disorder.** Thus:

- Marriage will not bring unity between a man and a woman but fighting, acrimony, divorce, pain, and suffering for all involved.
- Love will not bring contentment to each other but disappointment.
- Submission will not bring selfless service to one another but abuse, based on seeing each other as inferior.
- The enemy as the Father becomes the enemy as the Dictator, the Policeman, the Deadbeat Dad, and the No Need for Dad.

- Children are now not gifts from the enemy, but accessories that quickly get in the way when parents want to pursue their freedom.

We always work to reintroduce formlessness and void back into the enemy's domain. Marriage today is providing a wonderful platform upon which to do that: High divorce rates, abuse, instability in the home, and economic uncertainty all contribute to undermining people's confidence in the enemy's design for marriage and the family.

Those who follow the enemy often forget that our Dark Lord is the Prince of this planet. Those who do not follow the enemy don't know that small detail about Who (His Darkness be praised!) is running this planet. Our Dark Lord is the Lord of Chaos, and under His rule, instability reigns. Ignorance of His operation is bliss. We need to keep humans stupid and happy.

Serve up the chaos and we serve our Dark Lord.

To: Baal-Kobalt <capturetheplanet@brimstone.com>

From: Wormwood <burnbabyburn@gothell.com>

Subject: Chaos and christians...a winning combo

Hey BK! That blasted book is the blueprint for marriage and the family. If pastors do not preach the whole book and people hear only bits and pieces of its message, they'll fill in the gaps with the culture's ideas.

People will think that they're being more realistic, more on top of how things "really are." Pastors can be lured into this "Get Real!" thinkin' just like everyone else.

But that idiot Paul tells Timothy how to lead his flock: "Preach the word; be instant in season, out of season; reprove, rebuke, exhort with all long suffering and doctrine. For the time will come when they will not endure sound doctrine; but after their own lusts shall they heap to themselves teachers, having itching ears; And they shall turn away their ears from the truth, and shall be turned unto fables. But watch thou in all things, endure afflictions, do the work of an evangelist, make full proof of thy ministry." [63]

But I like fables and unsound doctrine. Whew! I am glad to see not every pastor listens to Paul. That book needs to be tucked in the pew, not in the heart. It should gather dust not trust.

To: Wormwood <burnbabyburn@gothell.com>

From: Baal-Kobalt <capturetheplanet@brimstone.com>

Subject: Prepare ye the way of the Dark Lord's Man!

Good point. Our ultimate goal, of course, is to prepare the world for our Man of Action, or what that disdainful book calls the "Anti-Christ."

By destabilizing the family, and having fathers disappear, human beings are left with a hole in their psyches. They need a father-figure, a role model, someone to look up to and someone to emulate. Humans need to feel protected. They need to feel that they are important to their parents and to the future of this world.

Fathers in a family provide that. The enemy as father equally provides that. Stability and security are an expression of love. But without this kind of stability, this kind of love, humans will desperately search for it. Humans need someone to tell them they are worthy of being here.

With all the chaos we are creating in marriage and in families, this chaos provides the perfect stage for our Man of Action to take over. He is coming soon. He will be embraced by:

- Women: Abusive, cold or unloving husbands will provide a nice contrast to our Man, for he will be kind, loving, forgiving and sexy, unlike the dolts sitting at home or in prison or who are nowhere to be found;
- Young men: Absentee or harsh fathers, who didn't give their sons the approval they so desperately sought, will be so unlike our Man, for he will give them a higher purpose, lavish approval on them and will be caring and engaged like their fathers should have been;
- Young women: Fathers who didn't make them feel loved or having been subjected to the endless parade of Mom's boyfriends, who never took an interest in them or took too much interest (you know what I mean) will be so unlike our Man, for he will be a gentle, guiding, approving father-figure, who will radiate love to their hungry souls;
- Men: Guys who are looking for answers and a robust leader will find it in our Man; He is not a mothering softy like the enemy's son, as he is now being portrayed in modern churches;
- Children: Our Man will be someone who is always there, who will not disappear or be in and out of their lives all the time. He will be consistent and caring, providing emotional security without reservation.

When that book calls our Man the "Anti-Christ," we do not considered that an insult in the Dark Kingdom. We know He will be a counterfeit to the enemy's son. Our Man will not only go against the enemy's son but He will **replace** the son. He will receive all the love, devotion and worship that the son should get. I can hardly wait for our Man to arrive.

> To: Baal-Kobalt <capturetheplanet@brimstone.com>
>
> From: Wormwood <burnbabyburn@gothell.com>
>
> Subject: A lesson from history

Hey BK! In Evil Academy, we had a whole session on one of the Dark Kingdom's finest, Hitler. I forgot the details. But, I think he's a great example of this anti-Christ thing.

Help me out here.

> To: Wormwood <burnbabyburn@gothell.com>
>
> From: Baal-Kobalt <capturetheplanet@brimstone.com>
>
> Subject: With malice towards all

Yes, Hitler is a prime example of being an anti-Christ. He provides a grand blueprint of our Man of Action. Our Man, however, will exceed everything Hitler did, of course.

The destabilizing force in Germany was World War I. Many fathers never came back from that four-year long war. Those who did were devastated by it. They came home shell-shocked. Some were missing limbs or had shattered bodies. Their minds were tormented by their experiences. Many were helpless. Their sons looked at them with horror, pity and confusion. Their once strong soldier-fathers returned home defeated men.

Hitler capitalized on this with his Master Race idea. He wanted to create an army of beautiful, physically perfect men who were destined to lead their nation. They were trained in Hitler's philosophy (ours, actually) and were promised the whole world. These men along with Hitler controlled all areas of German society: family, marriage, the church, the courts and soon, life and death itself.

Hitler led Germany without apology or mercy.

Hitler was a father-figure, and everyone adored him. Women swooned in his presence. Men hailed him and felt proud to be German once again. Children sang his praises and were taught that he was the savior of his people.

The Dark Kingdom helped to inspire his transformation from a leader to a Messiah-like figure, whose noble task it was to clear Germany of its Jews. This unquestioning adoration of Hitler allowed him and his followers to inaugurate the most important part of the Dark Lord's agenda: the extermination of the enemy's Chosen People. Many years after World War II was over, Hitler's henchman Adolf Eichmann was brought to trial and had no remorse for his crimes. He was proud of what he accomplished.

So were we. Still are.

During World War II, the Dark Kingdom helped to deceive the international community. Many nations did not want Europe's fleeing Jews cramming into their countries, so Hitler was able to carry out his plans with relatively little interference. A few brave souls did try to stop what we were doing in Europe, but we made sure they were disposed of quickly. We will do the same with the enemy's followers when our Man of Action rules the world.

The U.S. was instrumental in stopping Hitler. We won't let that happen again. Making the U.S. unable to respond to world crises is all part of the plan. Without the U.S., no real opposition will be present. The U.S. has the power, resources, and resolve to go out and stop whatever we are trying to do. By the time Our Man is ready, the U.S. will be a non-player.

Think of D-Day without the Allies and you see the brilliance of this. History is instructive. A lot of people don't seem to care or connect the past with today.

Those who follow the enemy and know history are no doubt lamenting the decline of the U.S. because they can remember the times when the U.S. actually stood for something. It acted out of a sense of moral obligation, based, of course, on that blasted book.

Everything we are doing is setting the stage for our Man. Disruption in marriage and family brings chaos right into the home. When humans are so busy with all the chaos in their personal lives, we are free to work in the larger sphere. We go unnoticed and unrecognized for what we are doing and who we are.

When the enemy's son came the first time, he invaded this war zone called Earth. He mounted a campaign against the chaos that we had created and that we still work hard to sustain. Look at his audacity:

- He healed the sick. He confronted disfiguring and destructive diseases with restoration and wholeness.
- He raged against hypocrisy. He decried hate parading as love and tyranny parading as concern.
- He breathed life into the dead. He disarmed our Dark Lord's greatest weapon against human beings…the permanent silence of the grave.
- He himself walked out of the tomb. He paid the wages of humanity's sin and established, once and for all, that hope was alive and death no longer had its sting.
- He promised to return. He reminded the Dark Kingdom its reign is on borrowed time.

- He sent his spirit. He returned as the comforter who filled and equipped his early followers to do what he had called them to do.
- He still sends his spirit. He is still indwelling and equipping his followers to go out and do what he has called them to do.

His order confounds our chaos. But we still seek victory. Every family we can destroy, especially the ones in the church, yields us more ground. With enough ground gained, we can take over.

> To: Baal-Kobalt <capturetheplanet@brimstone.com>
>
> From: Wormwood <burnbabyburn@gothell.com>
>
> Subject: Get real!

Hey BK! Thanks for the history lesson. Humans repeat it 'cause who they are deep inside doesn't change. Not if we can help it. I love using that book against the enemy's followers. Its verses should guide them, but I love twistin' 'em: followers and verses!

Here's my fave: "Wives, submit yourselves unto your own husbands, as unto the Lord. For the husband is the head of the wife, even as Christ is the head of the church: and he is the saviour of the body. Therefore as the church is subject unto Christ, so let the wives be to their own husbands in every thing. Husbands, love your wives, even as Christ also loved the church, and gave himself for it…So ought men to love their wives as their own bodies…For no man ever yet hated his own flesh; but nourisheth and cherisheth it, even as the Lord the church…Nevertheless let every one of you in particular so love his wife even as himself; and the wife see that she reverence her husband."[64]

I love to listen to what men are thinking when they hear such stuff coming out of the pulpit:

- *Yeah, right. Submission? Are you kidding? I take care of myself. If I don't, who will?*
- *Love my wife like the enemy's son loved the church? You've never met my wife!*
- *Love my wife as myself? I loathe myself, and think I am a worthless piece of fish-wrap. If I treat her based on how I see myself, she's in trouble!*
- *Oh, that's an impossible standard. I do the best I can, and if it's not good enough, tough beans.*

The women also get ticked off:

- *My husband is the head of this family? No way. I make more than he does. He needs to submit to me.*
- *Submit to my husband? He's a selfish son of a gun who would have me acting like a slave!*
- *I can't give my all to him. He'll up and leave me one day, and then where will I be with all that submission stuff?*

I love this. If the son's followers are not all-in, they'll kowtow to their own natures and the culture. The family and marriage are earthly pictures of heavenly principles. But if pastors don't preach all of that book, there's no real revelation. No power to live it out. No real restraint. That's my kind of church! My kind of nation!

To: Wormwood <burnbabyburn@gothell.com>

From: Baal-Kobalt <capturetheplanet@brimstone.com>

Subject: How about them kids?

How about those verses on raising children?

I love to paint a bright orange bull's-eye on: "Children, obey your parents in the Lord: for this is right. Honour thy father and mother; which is the first commandment with promise; That it may be well with thee, and thou mayest live long on the earth. And, ye fathers, provoke not your children to wrath: but bring them up in the nurture and admonition of the Lord."[65]

We want:

- Broken parents, broken children
- Unengaged parents, estranged children
- Absent parents, unprotected children

One absolutely delightful result of destabilizing the family is: Who is there to protect the children?

- *If Mom is at work and the children are unsupervised, the Internet is only one mouse-click away…*
- *If Mom brings home Boyfriend #3, and she has three teen-aged daughters, why should she worry? He's such a nice guy and he's willing to watch them…*
- *If Dad is gone, and the Coach is so nice and wants the son to come up to his cabin in the woods, why would Mom say no? He's such a nice man…*
- *That man on the Internet—he's says he's seventeen-- wants the daughter to meet him. Mom's too busy at work and Dad's too busy with his new family. One meeting can't hurt…*

Ever try to approach a baby elephant or baby grizzly bear? Your success is very limited with Mama around. You must first shoot the mother. Then the babies are vulnerable. Destroy the family and suddenly, the babies are vulnerable.

We like vulnerable.

> To: Baal-Kobalt <capturetheplanet@brimstone.com>
>
> From: Wormwood <burnbabyburn@gothell.com>
>
> Subject: Once again, that cursed book gets it right

Hey BK! This sounds like a page right out of our playbook: "This know also, that in the last days perilous times shall come. For men shall be lovers of their own selves, covetous., boasters, proud, blasphemers, disobedient to parents, unthankful, unholy, without natural affection, trucebreakers, false accusers, incontinent, fierce, despisers of those that are good, traitors, heady, high minded, lovers of pleasures more than lovers of God; Having a form of godliness, but denying the power thereof: from such turn away."[66]

With Mom and Dad too chaotic, too busy or just too unconcerned, the culture ends up raising the kids. Our kind of culture preys on and poisons children. America's getting there. If parents aren't into the enemy, they can't raise children who are either. Less teaching, less influence and more of us to make the culture toxic. Just the way I like it.

> To: Wormwood <burnbabyburn@gothell.com>
>
> From: Baal-Kobalt <capturetheplanet@brimstone.com>
>
> Subject: No remorse: just divorce!

Our overall project is chaos, giving our Man of Action room to work. Divorce is a tool we use to bring this into the lives of everyone concerned. It's not just the dissolution of a marriage of two adults; it involves the children, the grandparents and the extended family. The pattern of hurt, rejection and bitterness will influence future generations. Divorce is a kind of Hiroshima: All it takes is one "bomb," and the effects are long-reaching.

I have heard the cry in the hearts of many children, wanting to tell their parents what they really think, but won't. They don't want to add more hurt. Here is what I have heard:

Divorce is a mirage. It promises cool, refreshing water in a desert. You want a brand new life, away from all that conflict. But you will find that it is only the shifting heat of denial. This denial prevents you from facing the source of your real unhappiness: It isn't because of your spouse. It is your failure to be personally honest with yourself and seek personal change.

The sole purpose of marriage is not to make you happy. When hard times come, you should do everything you can to make your marriage work. If you think counseling is expensive, try a lawyer.

See the world though my eyes—not just your own. Don't assume your unhappiness is mine and that I see your marriage the way you do.

Divorce doesn't end your unhappiness. It just shifts where the discord will be: from your house to a new house. Battles will continue and the war will go on in everyone's lives for as long as we live.

Think about the future. Think about when we leave home, and ask yourself these questions: When you die, what will your legacy to us? Remember how you solved your problems at our expense? Who will come to important events in our lives? Will it be you? Will it be your ex? Will you make special events harder by who comes and who doesn't? Who will have the greater influence on our lives? Will it be you? The new spouse of your ex? Who will we most fondly remember? Who will give us away on our wedding day? Who will be there when the first grandchild arrives?

Your marital problem might be solved, but for us, it's only the beginning of a lifetime of discussions, arguments and a sense that the divorce really didn't solve anything.

If you claim you get along better than you ever have with your spouse after the divorce, we will ask (although not out loud) why you weren't able to do so while still married.

You will, over the course of our lives, need to periodically justify the divorce and why it is was necessary, which brings back the hurt into our lives. We may wonder (again, not out loud) why you married that person in the first place. This grieves us even deeper, because we know that without that parent, we would not be here.

Your new significant other will always be hard for us to reconcile in our minds. Why? It is hard to see our parent with someone else.

Once divorce occurs, it is hard to assess all the damage that it will initially cause and will continue to cause in the future for us.

Once the idea of divorce as a solution to marital problems becomes acceptable, then it sets a precedent for the future: In your marriage, are you experiencing any pain? Any unhappiness? Any problems? Then leave. Divorce isn't just a process—it becomes a way of thinking. How we think about life will always find its way into our actions. Commitment, perseverance, duty and love all derive from a willingness to set aside short-term personal happiness as the sum total of one's existence and think about the larger picture. If we think self, we will act self. If we think love, then we will act love.

The downside of divorce for the Dark Kingdom is many kids from such families go searching for meaning in their life and find peace and purpose in the enemy's son. The church becomes a new family. The hurt and pain of those years come under the healing touch of the enemy. We lose them, but we have so many more that we are destroying. Well, my wily WW, what do you think?

To: Baal-Kobalt <capturetheplanet@brimstone.com>

From: Wormwood <burnbabyburn@gothell.com>

Subject: Chaos is a lovely thing

Hey BK! Love it. Chaos a-plenty!

We learned in Evil Academy to set up a Chaos/Benefit Chart when we pester humans. Here's one for the choicest chaos:

Chaos	Benefits to the Dark Kingdom	Attacks the enemy's values
Suicide	Death is final; survivors live with guilt and unanswered questions; the pain never leaves them	"I am come that they might have life, and that they might have it more abundantly." (John 10:10)
Alcoholism	Destroys the person's body & mind; children and families destroyed; kids follow the pattern	"For the joy of the Lord is your strength" (Neh. 8:10)
Denial	The deep pain gets ignored so brokenness doesn't get dealt with	"And ye shall know the truth, and the truth shall make you free." (John 8:32)
Divorce	It's all about the self; easier to leave than to work on marriage; devastates children; moves the battleground; painful legacy	"'The man who hates and divorces his wife,' says the LORD, the God of Israel, 'does violence to the one he should protect,' says the LORD Almighty. So be on your guard, and do not be unfaithful." (Mal. 2:16)

Bring on the abuse! It mars the souls of children. These children grow up with the enemy's image on their soul blurred by pain, anger and a deep sense of loss. Sexual, physical, emotional, you name it—bruise the tender soul of a child and we benefit.

Cool, huh? There are more chaos bombs to toss in, but these are good ones.

Their pain, our gain.

To: Wormwood <burnbabyburn@gothell.com>

From: Baal-Kobalt <capturetheplanet@brimstone.com>

Subject: Let's go hunting

Well done. Sow chaos in people's lives and we reap the benefit. We assault people and those around them. We set up a pattern that keeps reverberating down through the generations, moving the Dark Kingdom forward.

Your training will serve you well as we go a-hunting into the churches, where we can target the christian family. Ah, the chaos there is multiplied. The enemy's book makes marriage a reflection of his relationship to his people, as we've discussed. Family equally reflects his presence in how the members are to treat one another.

We always use the enemy's words in a twisted way, just as His Darkness did with Eve in the Garden. Then all the Dark Lord had to do was wait, while Eve deceived Adam.

Let us start with women first: "Likewise, ye wives, be in subjection to your own husbands; that, if any obey not the word, they also may without the word be won by the conversation of the wives…"[67]

The culture is already dismantling these words. The culture now greatly influences how these words are interpreted by the church. People scornfully equate "subjection" with "abuse."

Armed with key verses from that deplorable book and a cultural interpretation of the biblical vocabulary, many a man believes he is the unquestioned head of the household and that his wife must submit to him. He acts like a tyrant and treats her as a slave. He's got that book, after all.

We applaud that attitude and encourage it whenever we can. In church or out of church, that book provides a delightful platform for a selfish man to stay selfish, because he varnishes his behavior with holy words. If anyone questions him or his behavior, especially the wife, he responds that he is following the book.

Such an attitude makes a christian home a prison and a christian marriage a lonely proposition. Such an attitude moves the Dark Kingdom forward.

The wife can equally use these words to denigrate herself, all in the name of her faith. She interprets them as it is her sole responsibility to win her husband to the enemy's kingdom. She thus allows him to treat her abominably in order to win him over. She is captured and imprisoned by such words. He continues to abuse her and she endures it. Because some day, she reasons, she will bring him to the enemy.

She misses or just ignores those verses that talk about how the enemy's spirit is the only one who changes people. It is not her responsibility to convert him. Only the enemy's spirit has the power to convict him of his sin.

Her behavior is to reflect her faith. Her prayers and her faith in the power of the enemy's spirit to do the work is her responsibility. She then is supposed to rest in the spirit.

But the truth of that gets lost under our watch. Our twisting of that book leads her down a heartbreaking road.

She thinks she is serving the enemy when in fact she is really enabling her husband to be a tyrant. A selfish man will not be grateful. He will act as if he deserves such treatment from his wife. But, he inwardly despises his wife for being weak. He equates her faith with weakness. He wouldn't want such a faith, now would he?

If her husband does follow the son, let him cherry-pick only those verses that allow him to not really change.

These verses, aimed at men, must be twisted as well: "Likewise, ye husbands, dwell with them according to knowledge, giving honor unto the wife, as unto the weaker vessel, and as being heirs together of the grace of life; that your prayers be not hindered."[68]

Can't you just hear this guy responding to such teaching: *You mean how I treat her will influence my praying and my relationship with God? Really?*

How about this one: "Husbands, love your wives, and be not bitter against them."[69] *You mean I can't rule over her to keep her in her place? You mean she is to be loved, and not commanded?*

And this one: "Husbands, love your wives, even as Christ also loved the church, and gave himself for it."[70] *I have to love her the way Christ loves me? Hey, he died for me and loved me even when I was a sinner. You mean, I have to give my all to her, even when I know she doesn't deserve it?*

When human nature goes up against the enemy's book and human nature wins, the Dark Kingdom advances. If we pervert the enemy's words and discourage pastors from preaching it in its fullness, then we will have a lot of people who skip down the road of tyranny in the enemy's name. It's a long and winding road we have prepared for them.

To: Baal-Kobalt <capturetheplanet@brimstone.com>

From: Wormwood <burnbabyburn@gothell.com>

Subject: That book

Hey BK! I remember Baal-Anarch once telling us that "A text without a context is a pretext." The enemy's words can be twisted, and it's awesome when it's the enemy's followers doing it!

People outside the enemy's kingdom are disgusted by it.

People inside? Unhappy. Big time.

If men use that book to abuse their wives, score one for us! Selfish men don't change, 'cause life's too good. If men claim to follow the son and then treat their wives like they don't, right on. If women let men hurt, beat and abuse them all in the name of being a "good christian woman," and they're doormats with the enemy's name stamped on 'em...well good for us.

It all just makes the enemy's followers look bad. Boo-hoo.

To: Wormwood <burnbabyburn@gothell.com>

From: Baal-Kobalt <capturetheplanet@brimstone.com>

Subject: All tangled up!

So true. Using that book to provide a veneer of respectability to sinful behavior always delights me.

We undermine the family, especially in the churches, by having the followers misuse that despicable book. If men do not see that their relationship with the enemy's son should permeate every part of their lives, especially in being good husbands and loving fathers, children grow up confused about what a father is.

We thus keep adding nails to the "enemy as father" coffin.

If women do not see themselves as children of a loving heavenly father, then they will go to the culture for validation. The culture is more than happy to make them feel ugly and unloved unless they look and act a certain way, which, of course, changes all the time. We are so thankful to "beauty" magazines and to popular media for how they make women loathe themselves.

Women who feel worthless will cling then to any men who make them feel even a tiny bit better.

We know men can be spiders. Women? They will be lost and lonely little flies, buzzing about with confusion and hurt. Right into the web they go!

Children? They will equate fatherhood with being abusive, inconsistent or simply not being there. Thus, the up and coming generation will not see any use for the enemy or his book. Just the way we like it.

To: Baal-Kobalt <capturetheplanet@brimstone.com>

From: Wormwood <burnbabyburn@gothell.com>

Subject: Bah on forgiveness!

Hey BK! Divorce is a great way to shatter the enemy's image, especially to church kids. Kids are going to believe more in the enemy because of what their parents do and say than what they hear in Sunday school. If what they hear in church isn't acted out at home, confusion kicks in. Say, for example:

- If following the enemy means forgiving one another, and one parent won't forgive the spouse when he or she blows it, or both parents nit-pick at each other's faults all the time, a child might wonder at their faith. Heck, a kid might even wonder if being a follower of the enemy makes any difference at all.

- If following the enemy means loving one another and parents are mean with each another, something doesn't add up. The enemy's love may not be real, 'cause a kid has a hard time seeing it in their parents.

- If following the enemy means dying to self, then a selfish parent will make a child wonder why that parent can't get it together. If that parent takes pride in following the enemy and is highly visible at church, but goes home and acts like everyone else for the rest of the week, that kid will be really confused. A confused kid can be an angry kid or even better, a confused kid might huck the whole faith thing out.

Added bonus: Schools teach kids that in this Darwinian world, life has no purpose or meaning. No surprise that kids grow up into angry and vengeful young adults. Mass murder, anyone? Suicide? Drug abuse? Despair?   Don't give a rip?

These kids are **lion chow.** Mom and Dad who say they follow the enemy but really don't, help move our Kingdom forward.

> To: Wormwood <burnbabyburn@gothell.com>
> From: Baal-Kobalt <capturetheplanet@brimstone.com>
> Subject: Bring on the Man!

Children served up to the Dark Kingdom are always a dainty and desirable treat.

We are going, for the last part of our review of how to undermine the family, to show how we must subvert that horrible 1 Corinthians 13. Love is what runs, sustains and characterizes all who are in the kingdom of the enemy.

Destroy his kind of love with our kind of "love" and we can bring marriage, family and church crashing down.

Before we unpack that nauseating chapter, let's quickly review a psalm that rankles me every time I hear it:

> Blessed is the man that walketh not in the counsel of the ungodly, nor standeth in the way of sinners, nor sitteth in the seat of the scornful.
>
> But his delight is in the law of the LORD; and in his law doth he meditate day and night.
>
> And he shall be like a tree planted by the rivers of water, that bringeth forth his fruit in his season; his leaf also shall not wither; and whatsoever he doeth shall prosper.
>
> The ungodly are not so: but are like the chaff which the wind driveth away.
>
> Therefore the ungodly shall not stand in the judgment, nor sinners in the congregation of the righteous.

> For the LORD knoweth the way of the righteous: but the way of the ungodly shall perish.[71]

Notice how the "ungodly," "sinners" and the "scornful" are everywhere, fomenting rebellion wherever they congregate.

If the "righteous." are to avoid being influenced by them, the righteous need to be planted elsewhere. The righteous must be planted in that book. The righteous then can flourish and be productive for the enemy. So, if we want to destroy that prospering tree, dam(n) up the stream.

Without that book to guide them, people will be drawn to the fun places where **our** people congregate. Children will gather there, too. The next generation will carry the torch of ignorance, rebellion and sin-loving behavior.

If the La-La Land of Chapter 13 of 1 Corinthians meets the Hard Road of Reality, then we can watch the whole thing derail. We can make a laughing-stock out of the enemy's kingdom and prepare this generation to hunger and thirst for a new way of thinking. Our Man of Action will provide just that.

Now, let's break down that nauseating chapter. The enemy sets high standards. But we know how these humans think, don't we? Let's fan the flames of pride and rebellion whenever they hear these verses. 1 Corinthians 13 is the constitution of the enemy's kingdom, because love should permeate every thought and action of his followers.

But, if we decimate his word, and let culture do the talking, we get followers who are confused on to how to think and act.

Let's imagine how his followers, taunted by us, will see these verses on love:

"If I speak in the tongues of men or of angels, but do not have love, I am only a resounding gong or a clanging cymbal."[72]

Hey, I go to church. I am kind to others when they deserve it. But if someone makes me angry, I am going to tell them what I think. If my spouse is acting stupid, I will tell her. What business is it of yours if I entertain myself with violence and sex? I'm not hurting anyone! So what if my kids watch what I watch? So what if they play the video games I play? They're just kids—they don't really get it anyway. I need my downtime.

"If I have the gift of prophecy and can fathom all mysteries and all knowledge, and if I have a faith that can move mountains, but do not have love, I am nothing."[73]

Yeah, I am smart and earn good money. I speak the truth and try to understand what's going on. I have faith, and yet, the world makes me so angry. I listen to talk radio and TV where people shoot down everyone and everything. I get anxious when I hear what's going on, and I let my angry words fly in front of my kids. I don't pray for those in leadership and my anger permeates my mood. Yeah, they know I believe, but when I am like this, they have a hard time seeing me walk by faith. I walk a lot by sight.

"If I give all I possess to the poor and give over my body to hardship that I may boast, but do not have love, I gain nothing."[74]

Hey, I am generous and I do a lot for the church. I help out and sometimes I am willing to go the extra mile. But, man, when I get home, I sure let the family know about how inconvenient it all was and talk trash about those involved with me. I even let slip a few unkind words about the pastor. My kids ask why I go then, and all I can say is that we're supposed to help out. Doesn't mean we have to like it, though.

"Love is patient, love is kind."[75]

So true, until your dad comes home late for the fifth time and I need to remind him of that. I expect my kids to say "please" and "thank you" to everyone, but to my husband? Nah—he needs to get his fat butt off the couch and help me carry in the groceries. If he helps out without me having to ask, well, I shouldn't have to thank him. He should do it anyway.

"It does not envy, it does not boast, it is not proud."[76]

*That's all well and good, but I don't earn what my spouse earns. She holds it over my head that her job is not only better than mine, it pays better. She thinks she can run the family because of her exalted position. She treats me like an inferior, and her pride suffocates me. It's all about her, her, her. Yeah, I know the kids cringe when they see us fight, but I will **not** be a doormat.*

"It does not dishonor others, it is not self-seeking, it is not easily angered, it keeps no record of wrongs."[77]

Porn—c'mon. It doesn't hurt anyone. She reads romance novels—isn't that a kind of porn? She doesn't know what I look at, and she doesn't need to know. Besides, as long as I keep it to myself, and make sure the kids don't see it, what's the harm? It's not like I am having an affair. Besides, all those times she's hurt me have made me not want to go near her. So, she's got her books and I've got my computer. The kids don't know—so don't pick on me.

"Love does not delight in evil but rejoices with the truth."[78]

I was so happy to see him get his comeuppance. He deserved to get fired. He went in late every day and I got so tired having to explain to the kids how their dad was not a loser—even though he clearly is. I was angry when the pastor spoke of women submitting to their husbands and men loving their wives as Christ loved the church. Yeah, I know it's in the Bible—but that was back in the day. Women today are equal in every way to men and there is no way my husband is going to be the leader of this home. Besides, he doesn't even go to church with me most Sundays. Our sons, a while back, said that religion is a woman's thing. I cringed—I told them it's for everyone. Yet, I do see more women than men in our church, and less and less men in leadership. I wonder if our sons will stop going once they are old enough?

"It always protects, always trusts, always hopes, always perseveres."[79]

Yeah, I know I need to be there for my children. I have a new family now, and with my job's demands, my kids get left in the dust. Besides, I can't stand my ex-wife's new boyfriend. He's a jerk and I don't let an opportunity go by where I don't tell my kids that. They seemed stressed; they say they approved of the divorce, because we were fighting all the time. In fact, I get along with my ex better than I did when we were married. They don't like my new wife. Yet, they say they are happy for me. I want to be there for them, and my ex's boyfriend around my daughter makes me uncomfortable, but it was my wife who wanted me to leave. Yes, we all still go to the same church—I sit there with my new family and she sits there with the kids and Mr. Jerk. I wanted it to work, but I got tired of the fighting. I hope the kids will be alright.

"And now these three remain: faith, hope and love. But the greatest of these is love."[80]

I guess, in some perfect world. When I sit in church on Sunday, and know of all of the divorced couples sitting there, including the pastor, I wonder: Are we losing this younger generation because what they hear and what they see aren't matching up?

Done and delightful. The kingdom of the enemy is built on love. Our Kingdom is built on hatred, acrimony and chaos. Ours is the easiest path and the quickest way, because we appeal to human nature. Humans hear of the enemy's love and try to embrace his promises. It takes time, discipline and a death to self to make love work.

We, on the other hand, have the stronger promise: You are in control and you shouldn't have to lie down and be a doormat for anyone, especially your spouse. You will be happier if you focus on you.

With narcissism flooding in and immersing the culture into murky waters, we can drown people in the church.

But, if the son's followers are like that irritating Noah, we have a problem. Look at what Noah did. He built an ark to house and provide for his family under the directions of the enemy. He survived the flood because he was obedient. Was that easy? No. People mocked him and all those animals...what a mess.

Yet, despite the hardship, he and his family prevailed. Why? He literally stood on the enemy's promise of salvation. The enemy closed the door of the Ark. Noah did what he needed to do and the enemy did what he promised to do. Noah and his family were preserved in those turbulent times by their faith and obedience.

We will keep the waters churning without mercy for as long as we can—sweeping away families, churches and all those promises the enemy makes.

The U.S. with all of the chaos we are bringing to the family, the nation and the churches is being prepared for our Man, as you well know.

If the people are standing on shifting sand, anyone promising a firm foundation will be seen as a savior.

That blasted book provides bedrock. People who stand on it will not be swept away. Our task then is to shatter it, hide it, deride it--do whatever you must do. We are nearing a time when the enemy's kingdom and the Dark Kingdom will collide.

We must be vigilant in preparing the people, both followers and non-followers, **to be deceived.** Their hearts must grow cold towards all things of the enemy, his values, and his book.

Go forth, my wicked Wormwood.

Please file a progress report in 66 days.

We are eager to hear of your work in bringing our darkness to the enemy's light.

NSA Release No. 4

Contents:
- Document #1: Letter from Daniel to the Saints
- Document #2: Transcript of The Dark Lord's Commencement Speech to Wormwood's Graduating Class
- Document #3: Letter from Gabriel to the Saints

Document #1: A Letter from Daniel

To: The Blessed Ones of His Calling
From: Daniel
Subject: How we gathered the following material

    We continued to monitor Wormwood's activity in conjunction with a large number of other demons who have received training at each of the various Malevels.
    We then infiltrated a large graduating ceremony many months later. It was larger class than other ones in recent memory.
    I, once again in utter devotion to our wonderful Heavenly King, went incognito and recorded the graduation speech given to this unusually large gathering of demons. It is no surprise that the Dark Lord wants to release utter havoc upon the United States and upon Christian churches in particular.
    Our precious Lord's presence in the churches today is the only impediment to the Dark Lord and his demons completely overrunning the United States. It is of great concern to the Kingdom of the Almighty King that more and more churches are compromising the Word by preaching a diluted or abbreviated form of the Gospel.
    Our Eternal Father dwells where His Son is lifted up, where His children are justified by the blood, and where His

saints walk in obedience to His Word. But today, in many churches, His Word is being replaced by a culturally relevant "gospel."

Paul faced the same incursion of untruth into the Gospel message.

Inspired by the King's Spirit, he said,

> I marvel that ye are so soon removed from him that called you into the grace of Christ unto another gospel: Which is not another; but there be some that trouble you, and would pervert the gospel of Christ. But though we, or an angel from heaven, preach any other gospel unto you than that which we have preached unto you, let him be accursed. As we said before, so say I now again, if any man preach any other gospel unto you than that ye have received, let him be accursed. For do I now persuade men, or God? or do I seek to please men? for if I yet pleased men, I should not be the servant of Christ. But I certify you, brethren that the gospel which was preached of me is not after man. For I neither received it of man, neither was I taught it, but by the revelation of Jesus Christ. [81]

Paul was inspired to write to another church,

> But I am afraid that as the serpent deceived Eve by his cunning, your thoughts will be led astray from a sincere and pure devotion to Christ. For if someone comes and proclaims another Jesus than the one we proclaimed, or if you receive a different spirit from the one you received, or if you accept a different gospel from the one you accepted, you put up with it readily enough... And what I am doing I will continue to do, in order to undermine the claim of those who would like to claim that in their boasted mission they work on the same terms as we do. For such men are false apostles, deceitful workmen, disguising themselves as apostles of

Christ. And no wonder, for even Satan disguises himself as an angel of light. So it is no surprise if his servants, also, disguise themselves as servants of righteousness. Their end will correspond to their deeds. [82]

These words reverberate down through the ages. We face more than ever "another gospel." Such an embrace of any other gospel will lead people to walk in darkness.

Where darkness is embraced, the Lord of Light will remove His Presence. A church without His guiding and empowering Spirit will become a white-washed tomb: beautiful on the outside (pleasing to men) but filled with the bones of the dead (displeasing to the Lord).

Please, dear saints, as you read this transcript of the graduation speech, please remember: we are at war.

Our glorious King needs leaders, not followers; soldiers, not pacifists; and doers, not just hearers, of His word.

Servant of the Most High,

Daniel

Chief Operations Angel to the Western World
North America Operations
Dominion: United States of America

Document #2: The Graduation Speech

"I, the Dark Lord, wish to commend you. You have trained well. You now have a deeper knowledge of the inner workings of the Dark Kingdom. Just as the enemy's kingdom wants his followers to grow in their knowledge and understanding of his ways, we wish you to know more of Ours. Therein lies your power.

The enemy rested after assembling this despicable planet. He placed his children in a garden with a cosmic gamble: These beings could either believe in him or reject him. Love cannot be coerced. I knew this. I, of course, prefer rape of the soul, and love cowering in fear. But not so with the enemy.

After the enemy was finished with his creation, I showed up as a snake. I blended in to the very Tree Eve was commanded to avoid.

If I had showed up as a lovely singing bird in that tree or as a flitting butterfly, going from branch to branch, then Eve would have sensed that the voice she heard was quite separate from her own.

I knew this as well.

I always work subtly at first—a hint here, a whisper there. Once I establish a base of operations, I go for the jugular. I knew this. Adam and Eve did not.

My voice, coming softly from within the branches, was able

to blend in with her own imaginings. At moments, the ideas seemed to come from her. Her thoughts and My whisperings danced to the music of pride, drowning out the enemy's warnings.

If you appeal to humans' pride, you will have them eating from any forbidden tree they encounter.

Why? Pride is just another word for "deity." Tell stupid humans: You can be your own god: in control, calling the shots, meting out punishment and expecting utter devotion.

I ought to know. I was accused of having pride. I was dismissed from Heaven because the enemy would not share the running of the whole universe with his Peer.

Why not? I was equally qualified to be Lord Over All. I did ultimately get what I wanted: I am now the Prince of this world, the Lord over this Earth. I have My Kingdom and I am ruling it now. Of course, I wanted the whole universe. I wanted to run it forever according to My way of thinking. [sigh]

The enemy's model of love is ridiculous. My ideas on how to run things were then, and still are, far superior.

I got the Earth. Yes, it is true I have it for a limited time. Oh, but what a time I have had all these years! What a time still remains for us!

You are a part of My Dark Army, going forth and conquering with Me.

So, armed with knowledge of how the enemy had set up his creation--based on humans choosing what his divine love offers--I was able to throw the whole creation into disarray. I made Eve doubt her understanding of what the enemy said; I manipulated her to exchange the enemy's knowledge for Mine. I offered her the best kind of knowledge: by knowing good from evil, she and Adam would be like their creator!

Here's the beauty of this: The promise of **being like the enemy** can soon transform into **being the enemy.**

The enemy wants his children to be like him: choosing love, offering forgiveness, practicing charity and demonstrating concern.

But My knowledge, whispered into every human's ear since that encounter in the Garden has been:

*Why just **follow** him? Why not just **be** him?*

*If you are capable of being him, who **needs** him? You have **you!***

*You have the knowledge deep **within your divine self—go forth and conquer this planet.** You can be your own god: your wisdom, your knowledge and your actions will be enough.*

Don't allow some distant outside force to control you! Step up yourself!

Appeal to human pride with glorious promises, and success is guaranteed.

Sometimes, it is too easy. But there is beauty in such simplicity.

The enemy bestowed intelligence into these humans, of which imagination is an important component. If humans can **think** it, **imagine** it, then humans **can do it.**

Adam and Eve listened to My logic. Their rebellion stripped away their innocence of what evil is and does. Adam and Eve's bite on that forbidden-knowledge-fruit poisoned humanity's imagination from that time forward. A corrupted imagination coupled with My whispered knowledge is a powerful tool. I can step back and watch evil bloom.

Adam and Eve's very own son acted quickly using this new tool. Cain was driven by pride, envy, rage and then, sweetest of all, murder. Cain could enviously think about Abel's preferential treatment and imagine what life would be like without him. He pondered how wonderful it would be not to have such a simpering brother around whose behavior was so sickeningly obedient.

Just keep thinking about it, Cain: *What if that idiotic Abel weren't around?*

It's not hard for humans to commit evil after the imagination has been on overdrive.

Abel's blood was a sweet offering on the altar of the Dark Kingdom. Cain's thinking and then acting upon his imaginings was the first catastrophe in a long march of death down through the millennia. We stand on the sidelines, cheering as the atrocities, genocides, murders and rapes march in tune with sinful minds and poisoned imaginations year after year, century after century.

Even humans will admit that "A little knowledge is a dangerous thing." In fact, a little is all that is needed to send the enemy's children into the abyss.

This is your calling, My Dark Army. You are to set in motion evil at every opportunity. [huge applause]

You have no bodies but you do have the minds of the enemy's children to inhabit and their hands and feet to carry out our agenda. Our goal? Humanity's destruction. Pure and simple. I don't want humanity wallowing in sin. I want them drowning in it. [huge applause]

I want the vices they crave to be poison to their souls. I want them going on their merry way, down to the grave showing no repentance, no remorse, and no acknowledgment that sin costs a lot!

Death is the ultimate price they pay.

I want them to feel throughout their lifetimes that everything they thought and did was right.

I so enjoy hearing the first words many humans utter entering My Hell: *"It is real!"*

My greatest trump card has always been the grave. No matter how prideful people are, everyone trembles before the silence and permanency of death. Rich or poor, child or adult, male or female—all cower before this overwhelming Unknown. Its finality, its no-second-chances, and its coldness take humans by the throat and terrorizes them.

Until that day the enemy's son showed up.

I knew he would appear one day. The enemy's declaration that the son would one day bruise My head was bitter to Me. I wanted so much to derail the enemy's creation in that Garden. I wanted victory and I wanted it to be permanent. But upon hearing those words about the son's victory, I vowed to do everything I could to strike the son's heel. Over and over again.

I, your Dark Lord, Who had been thrown out of Heaven and was no longer able to taunt the enemy, decided to go after his dearly beloved humans without ceasing. Every generation would hear My whisperings without fail. [applause]

I would wait for his son. In the meantime, I maliciously pursued the enemy's creation, bringing forth every evil I could.

I used my trump card with Adam and Eve: **One bite of the fruit led to the bite of the grave forever!** With Adam and Eve so swayed, I was victorious over the enemy. Adam and Eve and all of their descendants went into the dust, the very element that I was cursed to slither through. I didn't care: I had them where I wanted them: decaying in the cold hard ground. [applause]

But then, the enemy's son left the courts of heaven, and wrapped himself in the very flesh I am always seeking to destroy. He entered this miserable creation of his father's and went to work. Why would anyone want to become like the enemy's children? I have no answer to that.

My plans to forever derail humanity were threatened.

Once the son was placed in the manger, I went right to work, enraging Herod. I goaded him with the thought that a new king would take over his rightful throne. One poisonous whisper and the heavens rang with the screams of terrified mothers and dying babies.

The enemy and I contended mightily that night. His son managed to escape the slaughter.

So many times I tried to destroy the son, but to no avail.

Until one day, Judas came up for sale, as it were. He was angry that the son hadn't used his power to overthrow the Romans.

I suggested to Judas that **he** turn him over to the authorities, to force the son's hand. Judas found this newly whispered idea too seductive to ignore: *If this Messiah can feed thousands, walk on water and raise the dead, then overthrowing the Romans would be child's play, right, Judas?*

Besides, doesn't your sacred text foretell of a conquering

Anointed King who will reign over his enemies? Your actions, Judas, will remind Jesus of his real purpose: to establish his kingdom on earth, with the Romans subjected to utter humiliation. You know, Judas, it's only fair: tit for tat on these barbarian rulers.

Enough with the healings and the teachings. This closeted warrior Messiah needs to throw off the trappings of a humble carpenter's son and go forth, without mercy, to cast the Romans into utter darkness.

The days of being nice are over, Judas. Only you understand the deeper mission of Jesus: to overturn the existing order and establish his rule. Isn't he always taking of the "Kingdom of God"? Enough talk.

Action is what is now needed, and you, Judas, will be instrumental in making this new kingdom burst forth from the shadows and burn brightly in the light of a new day!

I helped Judas forget why the son came. Jesus said that he came to give his life as a ransom for humanity—to pay the ultimate debt that the remission of sin demands. He would be the perfect sacrificial lamb, whose split blood would, once and for all, cleanse the people and bestow divine forgiveness.

I, with a mere whisper of how unfair the son was being with his immense power, swept Judas away on an imaginary tour of Jesus versus the Romans, with Judas (of course) being the captain of the Lord's army.

Stupid Judas. His daydreaming was so off the mark.

Seeing Jesus arrested, beaten and scourged was more than his petty little conscience could take. The Dark Kingdom applauded as he swung from that tree.

Unfortunately, the Dark Kingdom didn't see how powerful the son truly was.

He would die for humanity—we understood that part. Our minions did their best to beat Jesus to death before he got to that cross. We wanted him to smash face down on that Jerusalem street and die right there. But no. Some loser, a Simon of Cyrene, carried his cross to the hill.

I was striking at his heel at every chance I could that day of his execution. [applause]

I again contended mightily with the enemy over the life of his son. [applause]

We scattered his followers. We whispered in their ears: *The Messiah is not supposed to die! This is all a mistake! Evil has won out! The Romans are coming for you next!*

Away they went—to hide away in small rooms. [applause]

I was especially pleased when Peter denied Jesus. I suggested he do what any self-respecting betrayer of someone so innocent should do: hang himself. I was elated with my success with Judas; but, I was not able to overcome Peter's horror at self-slaughter.

Then that third day arrived. Death, My final power over humanity, was broken.

Death itself could not hold this son.

The Dark Kingdom was appalled. What I thought was our final victory over the enemy and his son was overturned and replaced with empty grave clothes, an open tomb and a son who walked and talked again with his followers.

He took victory away from death. [hissing]

He took away its sting. [more hissing]

He was fully restored and fully victorious. [hissing]

Over sin. [hissing]

Over death. [loud hissing]

Over the Dark Kingdom. [very loud hissing]

So, My Dark Army, your greatest retaliation to this victory of the enemy's son is to let Death storm the planet, sweeping away as many as you can. Overwhelm these humans with wars, rumors of wars and false Christs who come only to deceive.

Incite nation to rise against nation, and kingdom against kingdom. Bombard the planet with famines, pestilences, and earthquakes, all leaving devastation in their wakes.

Begin the sorrows! [huge applause]

Persecute without mercy the son's followers. Make his followers hated with so much passion that they become fearful. To save their own skins, they will start to betray and hate each other.

Bring on an ever-increasing army of false prophets, whose very words will lead to even more confusion and chaos. Let these false prophets rise up in abundance and deceive many. Let their preaching be done in the name of love and tolerance for everyone!

Except those who follow the son, of course. They will get less and less mercy as time goes on. [applause]

Let the love of even the son's followers grow cold, as chaos and sin grow rampant. This is the way of the Dark Kingdom: coldness towards one another and coldness towards the enemy.

Grief is such a lovely thing: People look for a reason for their suffering and the enemy provides the perfect target for their ever-increasing rage when easy answers elude them. [applause]

Stir up global chaos. Create chaos in the heart and mind of every human. Create a planet filled with Cains and Abels.

Dismantle the claims the enemy makes to those who are searching for truth. You must whisper to them that not believing in God or Jesus' atoning death is a sign of intellectual superiority.

Dismantle the claims the enemy makes to those who believe. Show them that God's sovereignty is tantamount to him causing suffering, including taking people away "to a better place."

Or portray him as a passive spectator to all that suffering.

It's effective either way because belief becomes blame, blame become bitterness, and bitterness becomes alienation.

Blame the enemy for everything—especially those things that have come from the minds and actions of humanity itself.

Blame the enemy for death, destruction, disease and disorder. Make the enemy's sovereignty equal to tyranny or carelessness.

One poisonous whisper can work wonders in the hearts of non-believers or believers, causing them to wonder and then doubt! [applause]

Start the smear campaign with these nagging whispers:

Isn't life like jumping from a plane with no parachute? It's exhilarating at first...with the wide blue sky above and the earth far below. But, as you get older and closer to death, you realize, hey, what if there really is no parachute? It's all made up. You are going to go "splat." You will land into darkness. Into nothing. There is no life after death. There is no hope.

Isn't life more in line with that Job guy of the Old Testament? He suffered utter loss: everyone and everything was taken from him. His suffering was tremendous and his loss was beyond imagining. How could you possibly accept that a loving God would do or allow such a thing?

Isn't life like a cruise ship that is eventually going to sink? Everyone plans to have a good life, gets ready and sets sail. Then this cruise ship runs aground and sinks, killing many passengers. The ones who survive feel totally misled: Life is supposed to be a glorious time; instead, many perish well before their time. Life can feel as if you have been gypped, duped or betrayed.

Isn't Death like a criminal? It is the ultimate Thief: You set up a beautiful house, reputation, wealth, only to have Death break in and steal it. Jesus observed the irony of placing too much emphasis on things that can be destroyed: "Do not store up for yourselves treasures on earth, where moths and vermin destroy, and where thieves break in and steal. But store up for yourselves treasures in heaven, where moths and vermin do not destroy, and where thieves do not break in and steal. For where your treasure is, there your heart will be also." [83]

Life is not a cabaret, old chum. Think of the wealthy people who spend a lifetime acquiring money, sometimes to do real good in the world. How unfair it is to work your whole life, only to walk out with nothing. Many people grow up poor; spend their whole life trying to get ahead, only to die at the end. Many good people, who honestly seek to benefit mankind, end up the same as the serial killer: dead.

Why must you be left alone when those you love are taken away from you? You will never see your loved ones again. Your relationships are so important to you. Is this really the end? Will those you love only turn to dust?

What if you cannot be by the bedside and say good bye?

What if there is no body to bring home? How can you mourn properly?

What if there is no gravesite to visit? It's so utterly unfair.

If people must die, why can't they just go to bed one night, and fall asleep?

Why must people be brutally killed?

Why must children suffer unspeakable things before death?

Why must torture even have to exist?

Why must people starve to death?

Why must they die from horrendously painful diseases?

Why? Why? Why? Death is scary enough, but when you consider how some people die, it's too chilling to even think about.

    Now, let us add in the notion that Hell is an antiquated idea and has no business being believed by a modern person.
    Heaven can be equally thought of as a child-like notion, where pets and Grandma go. But a real place? Get real.

But we know better. Hell is real. Heaven is real. Why? If there is no Hell, then what awaits those who have escaped earthly justice?

- Hitler killed himself in his bunker before the Russian troops got to where he was. Himmler, his right hand man, killed himself as well, thereby avoiding trial. Most Nazis, with the blood of millions on their hands, never were caught, let alone tried for their crimes.
- What about those mass shooters who will never go court, having been shot down in a gun battle with police, or killed themselves right after the rampage?
- What about the rapist who goes to trial but is not convicted for lack of evidence?
- What about the child molester who never gets caught and then dies…leaving behind an emotional debris trail of broken lives and murdered innocence?
- Death for these folks is an escape, away from the judgment and reach of earthly law. Their death is a "Get Out of Jail Free" card if Hell doesn't exist.

If there is no Heaven, then where do the innocent go?

- Where did the 1.3 million children who perished in the Holocaust go?
- Millions have died in abortion, famines, disease, murder and neglect. Their lives were snuffed out. Where are they now? Somehow having the innocent and the guilty vanish into nothingness cheapens life itself. If people are simply worm food, then how is life special in any way?
- Letting someone go would be horrible if you believe you will never see them again.
- Someone dies in agony. Is that truly it? They

checked off the planet in pain, only to go into the cold ground. They are beyond comfort and the cold earth seems such an inhospitable place to end up.
- Most victims never receive justice. Death makes sure of that: If there is no justice here, there's no justice ever.

But we know better. We know, My Dark Army, that the very presence of Heaven and Hell affirm life here on this miserable planet.

Without Heaven and Hell, life's injustice is far too overwhelming for humans to contemplate.

Our very purpose is this: destroy any credibility the enemy might have. Hell's gates swing wide open for the confused, the embittered, the angry, and the lost.

We want to undermine the very life-affirming aspects of Hell's presence.

How does Hell affirm life now and in eternity?

The enemy doesn't send people to hell. It's a choice that they have made. If someone doesn't love the enemy here, why would he grab that person at their death and force them to live with him forever? It would be a kind of divine rape: violating the heart of someone who didn't want to be with the enemy on earth but has to endure him for eternity, is appallingly unjust. Love by definition cannot be forced.

The enemy will not force himself on the very children he created.

Love rules the universe, much to My disgust. The enemy created the Cosmic Gamble: his creatures can choose to love him or hate him. He is constrained by his own design.

Sin entered humanity through Adam, and it has polluted humanity ever since. No one is perfect—we know that all too well. Humans love to compare themselves to each other and thereby declare with overweening pride that they are "good."

But the enemy is the standard. So, people fall short every time. Everyone stands equally inadequate before the enemy.

All are equally condemned, but all are equally offered the gift of salvation.

Hell is the place people choose to go by their beliefs and the behaviors that resulted from those beliefs. If they choose to live an earthly life without the enemy, they will equally live an eternal life without him.

Everyone will face a Higher Court of Law when it convenes. The Judgment will be fair and impartial because the judge (our enemy, and humanity's advocate) is that way.

No technicalities, no dream team of lawyers working the system for the benefit of the guilty. No injustice meted out. Only a fair verdict will be rendered.

Those who sought Hell, by rejecting the enemy's son, will not be denied.

Those who sought Heaven, by accepting the son into their hearts, will not be denied.

The enemy is fiercely loving but fiercely just. He balances the two on the scales of his love.

The enemy doesn't send people to Our gates. People send themselves.

How does Heaven affirm life now and in eternity?

The blind will see and the lame will walk. There are no wheelchairs in heaven. People will be completely restored: free to laugh, dance and sing. All pain and agony will be forgotten. With Heaven, those left behind cannot help but rejoice for those who leave.

All children will gather around the son and he will bless them. He blessed them here without reservation; there will be no different.

His creation reveals him as creator and his son reveals him as father. Seeking, asking and knocking means that if someone actively pursue him, they will find him.

Heaven is for those who came to really know him. Because all fall short of the enemy's glory, no one can do anything to be good enough.

Heaven is a gift, freely offered by the enemy's son, with his nail-scarred hands open to everyone.

Heaven's presence humbles these humans. People will invest not only in loving others, but also in praying, sharing and encouraging others about the life to come. People will live and raise children with eternity in mind. People will invest their lives helping others to see that while the here and now is precious, so is eternity.

When death takes away loved ones, people will say, "Until we meet again."

"Good-bye" is not in the vocabulary of Heaven.

Heaven is the place where all the needs of human beings will be forever met. There will be no more tragedy or pain—it is a place of reconciliation with the enemy.

His creatures are really returning back to the Garden.

Minus Me, of course.

That's why death-bed confessions don't bother the enemy—it is better to launch into an eternity with him even after a lifetime of ignoring him, than to live a full life and leave it for an eternity without him.

Heaven and Hell affirm life. Life is much more than what people suffer here. There is a life to come. Suffering will be over, justice will be served, and fairness will reign over all.

I know what you must be thinking, My Dark Army. It sounds as if we will lose this war against the enemy and his creation.

Yes, it is true: the end of the book has been written. Armageddon, despite its bloodbath, will result in the defeat of My Babylon: the City whose thrills kill.

Ah, but let not your hearts be troubled. We will raise as much Hell on earth as we can in the time remaining! [thunderous applause]

It's that love/choice thing all over again: the enemy is patiently waiting for people to seek, ask, knock and eventually choose him.

He has not brought down judgment for the iniquity that rules the earth now, for he waits with merciful patience. While he is waiting, we work with no holds barred.

Let me close with a story.

A missionary, serving in India, was awakened one night by his terrified daughter, who said that a giant snake was in the house. The missionary cautiously searched the house, and sure enough, a giant python had crawled in and was now menacing his daughter. He quickly grabbed his gun and placed a bullet squarely in the head of that python.

That should have been the end of it.

But no: that python was not going down so easily or peacefully. It started thrashing about and its long muscular body starting mowing down furniture. It continued thrashing and started taking out walls and windows.

By the time its death throes were over, the missionary's whole house was in ruins. He was safe; his daughter was safe. But their house was completely destroyed.

Start thrashing, My Dark Army. The enemy's son put a bullet in Our head that day on the cross. But we will not leave easily or peacefully. We will thrash this planet and destroy as many people as we can. We will unleash utter ruin and not stop until we must. [huge applause]

You now have a call to march forward, with all the power of Hell behind you.

Release utter destruction everywhere you can.

The son's appearance is at hand. His followers need to be divided, misguided and broadsided as often as you can and by whatever means necessary.

Our sons of disobedience should be seen as progressive, emerging thinkers who want christianity to have better branding. Work in the churches. Make them the kind of places I like to visit. I am always free on Sundays.

Encourage believers to dilute, refute and then not "give a hoot" about that enemy's book. Schmooze, confuse and then lose this generation, completely alienated from the enemy.

Time is short. Eternity is long.

I have a future date with the Lake of Fire, but until then, I am free.

Thank you. [thunderous applause]

Document #3: Letter from Gabriel

To: Those called by the King of Glory to be in His Mighty Army
From: Gabriel, Herald to the King of Glory
Subject: Commentary on the speech

It is disturbing to read how viciously the minions of the Dark Lord see the church and God's followers. It is equally disturbing to see how well demons know the Scripture.

Perhaps the followers of Jesus do not hear these demons' dark murmurings, for their lives are filled with distractions.

Perhaps His followers have grown complacent, no longer realizing just how prevalent these demons' dark workings are. People are struggling just with the challenges of every day and the chaos it brings.

The evening news, however, is a jarring reminder that larger forces are at work.

Many of His people think that better political leadership is needed. But people elect those politicians who reflect their values. Politics today show just how deep and acrimonious the divisions are over what those values should be. The nation's leaders and their failures are symptomatic of a larger problem: The nation is experiencing an ever widening chasm between those who follow God and those who don't.

The Dark Kingdom advances each day when God's people stand on the shifting sands of culture and the self, and not on the Rock of Our Savior and Lord, Jesus Christ and on the Word of God.

Politics are not the solution to this nation's woes. Christians should vote for people who stand on Biblical principles, but that alone is not sufficient. Revival for the nation does not start at the national level. It starts in the home. It starts when two people, as husband and wife, will commit to serving the Lord, each other and their family.

History is drawing to a close. Where will you be standing when God's righteous judgment comes?

The world now is in a time of grace, but God's justice will come.

In the meantime, let those who call upon His name serve as soldiers, in the service of our mighty King.

Our servant Paul extolled:

> Finally, be strong in the Lord and in his mighty power. Put on the full armor of God, so that you can take your stand against the devil's schemes. For our struggle is not against flesh and blood, but against the rulers, against the authorities, against the powers of this dark world and against the spiritual forces of evil in the heavenly realms. Therefore put on the full armor of God, so that when the day of evil comes, you may be able to stand your ground, and after you have done everything, to stand. Stand firm then, with the belt of truth buckled around your waist, with the breastplate of righteousness in place, and with your feet fitted with the readiness that comes from the gospel of peace. In addition to all this, take up the shield of faith, with which you can extinguish all the flaming arrows of the evil one. Take the helmet of salvation and the sword of the Spirit, which is the word of God.

And pray in the Spirit on all occasions with all kinds of prayers and requests. With this in mind, be alert and always keep on praying for all the Lord's people.[84]

Followers of the Mighty and Glorious King: Armor up!
Stay armored up and STAND.
Come, Lord Jesus.

Shalom,

Gabriel

Chief Herald of the Kingdom of Our Almighty King

Why This Book?

I know it's a bit odd to put an introduction at the end of a book. I wanted you, the reader, to fully listen in on the spiritual battle as "documented" in these pages, without having met the author in an introduction. Now, I will speak in my own voice.

I have walked in the Lord since I was 14. I am now 57. That doesn't necessarily mean anything—I could be a first-year christian 43 times over. But, because God is good and faithful, I have grown in my knowledge of Him throughout the years.

This book is a distillation of my experience as a Christian. I am ever-increasingly distressed at what I see going on in America right now.

Change happens and nothing in human affairs stands still. I understand that but when I see change happening that is detrimental to the church and to this country overall, it would be derelict of me to not comment.

Silence is either a sign of indifference or accommodation. I am not comfortable with either stance. So, what to do?

There are enough of pundits covering the political front.

There are plenty of bloggers debating the social and cultural scene.

There are plenty of Christian writers wrestling with the changes going on in the churches.

I wrestled with how I would enter the debate. One summer, as I was reading *The Screwtape Letters* by C.S. Lewis, it hit me: How about an updated version? I am not in C.S.

Lewis' league by any stretch, but I thought, Why not give it a go?

What you hold in your hands is that "go."

I loved writing this book, but it was painful to consider how the church has diluted the Gospel.

The amount of pain in the world is overwhelming.

As someone once said, "Hurt people hurt people."

I mean absolutely no disrespect to anyone. But even sincere people can be sincerely wrong. I see churches in America losing their Spirit-led power because of a willingness to embrace the culture and its values, all in the name of Jesus. Love and tolerance is seen as being the most important attributes of a modern church.

But, the most important attribute of all is missing: truth.

God's Word is not preached its fullness. Its power is diminished by only reading a few verses here and there, and focusing more on cultural relevance.

The power of the Word is diminished and consequently people's lives are not being changed under the skillful hand of the Holy Spirit.

Many churches seem to have the goal of making people feel welcomed and happy, so they will return Sunday after Sunday. It's as if we think that if a person simply sits in a church and hears the message, that person will become a Christian.

Does simply sitting in a baseball stadium make a fan a baseball player?

Does simply sitting in a classroom make a person a student?

No. God's word is clear: "Do not merely listen to the word, and so deceive yourselves. Do what it says."[85]

Are we in America on a spiritual *Titanic* with our thinking? We have a kind of "God Himself could not sink this ship" mentality about our country. We declare that we are a Christian nation, and that God will not allow America to suffer the fate of other nations who have turned their back on Him.

Even a cursory glance of the Old Testament shows that God will not be mocked endlessly by those who call upon His name, yet act disobediently to His commands.

So, I wrote this book with an unconventional slant, yes, but underneath the snide jabs and comments of the demons, is a voice crying out that we are entering a wilderness.

My voice.

But what I do I bring to the table in terms of qualifications?

The Holy Spirit inspired me to write this book.

I have a Master's Degree in Literature, and I have read a lot. I have also taught literature and writing for ten years in various scholastic and academic settings.

I eagerly devour books, especially history books.

In fact, it is history that drove me into the arms of Jesus.

In the 8th grade, I watched a movie in social studies about the Holocaust. I was stunned. How God could allow such an injustice made me angry at God. I declared myself an atheist. The problem was that if there is no God, then the Nazis literally got away with murder. It was that nagging thought that drove me to start a spiritual journey to find out who God was. (Atheism is truly sitting on the cosmic bench, eating your lunch alone. It's fine for a while, but after a while, you grow tired of being the only one speaking.)

I searched all of the world's religions and finally settled on Judaism, feeling that it had the best portrait of God. Then a friend of mine asked me to read the New Testament from a Jewish perspective, to see if Jesus was the promised Messiah or not. In my ignorance, I said I wouldn't read the New Testament, for it was written by Christians—non-Jews, in other words.

Soon after that, in middle school, we had to write about a famous person for an English project. I picked, yes, Jesus. I read every biography on Jesus I could find. By the time the project was completed, I was praying to God to help me find the best religion to please Him: either Judaism or Christianity.

One night, I placed a Star of David and a cross on my nightstand, hoping He would move the one I was supposed to follow by morning. He didn't of course, but before I fell asleep,

I prayed to Him and in my bedroom that night, I felt a peace and a warmth come over me. His presence has never left me. My search was over. My new journey had begun.

It is injustice and man's appalling behavior in times past and today that keep me following that One Who said that He is "the Way, the Truth and the Life." What more does a person need? More than ever, I see that humanity, above all else, needs a Savior. History shows me that time and time again. My own life does as well.

My prayer is that the Holy Spirit will call you to a deeper walk in Him. The days are darkening, and now, more than ever, we must be convinced of His truth in His Word. We are called to put on the armor of God, which implies this planet is a battlefield. I pray this book will be part of a spiritual boot-camp.

May God stir His people to arise in the power of the Spirit and go forth as good soldiers, who fight for Truth and desire greatly to run missions to the very gates of Hell.

One final comment. Satire is a bitter pill to swallow. We laugh, sometimes uncomfortably, but we laugh nevertheless. Why? Because satire isn't just about making you laugh. It is biting social commentary, housed in humor. So, I am sure there were times you were offended or shocked by the comments of the demons; I meant no disrespect to our Lord.

But we are not at a football game, cheering our team.

We are not at a political rally getting all worked up, only to go home andf become activists.

We are in a war. Whether we are prepared or not, the Gates of Hell are swinging wide open. God bless you, sweet saint. May we all armor up and go forth in His name and in the power of His love. Jesus is the answer.

Rhonda L. Thorne Cramer
Boise, Idaho
2018

Endnotes for the Biblical References

[1] Romans 8:11 NLT
[2] Acts 17:6 KJV
[3] 1 Pet. 2:9 NIV
[4] 1 John 4:8 NIV
[5] 2 Chron. 7:14 NIV
[6] John 16:33 NIV
[7] James 2:19 NIV
[8] Prov. 14:12 NIV
[9] 2 Tim. 2:16 NLT
[10] Gal. 3:28 KJV
[11] Deut. 8:3 NLT
[12] Deut. 8:17 NLT
[13] Eph. 2:14 NLT
[14] James 2:14-17 NIV
[15] Rom. 3:23 NLT
[16] Rom. 10:13-14 KJV
[17] Col.1:28 NIV
[18] Eph. 4:11-13 NIV
[19] 2 Tim. 2:15 NIV
[20] 2 Tim. 4:3-4 NIV
[21] Gal. 1:6-7 NIV
[22] Gal. 1:8-9 NIV
[23] 1 Cor. 3:11-13 NIV
[24] 1 Cor. 1:18 KJV
[25] Rom. 10:17 KJV
[26] Rom. 12:2 KJV
[27] Heb. 4:12 KJV
[28] 2 Cor. 3:18 NIV
[29] 1 Cor. 15:45 NIV
[30] Romans 6:6-11 NLT
[31] Romans 8:1-2 NLT
[32] Gal. 2:20 NIV
[33] 1 Cor. 2:8 NIV
[34] Psalm 40:2 NLT
[35] Heb. 12:15 NLT

[36] Matt. 7:21-23 NIV
[37] Gen. 11:4 NIV
[38] John 12:31 NIV
[39] 1 Pet. 2:21 KJV
[40] Heb.12:7 & 11 NIV
[41] Rev. 3:19 NIV
[42] 1 John 4:4 KJV
[43] Matt. 15:19 NLT
[44] 1 John 1:9 KJV
[45] Tozer, A. W. "This World: Playground or Battleground?"
[46] Tozer, A. W. "This World: Playground or Battleground?"
[47] Ephesians 6:10-20 NIV
[48] Eph. 6:13 NIV
[49] Eph. 6:14 NIV
[50] Eph. 6:14 NIV
[51] Eph. 6:15 NIV
[52] Eph. 6:16 NIV
[53] Eph. 6:17 NIV
[54] Eph. 6:17 NIV
[55] Eph. 6:18 NIV
[56] Heb. 12:1-2 NIV
[57] 2 Tim. 2:4 NIV
[58] Is. 54:5 KJV
[59] Rev. 19:9 KJV
[60] Hos. 2:19-20 KJV
[61] Hos.11:1 KJV
[62] Gen. 1:1 KJV
[63] 2 Tim. 4:2-5 KJV
[64] Eph. 5:22-5, 28-9, 33 KJV
[65] Eph. 6:1-4 KJV
[66] 2 Tim. 3:1-7 KJV
[67] 1 Peter 3:1 KJV
[68] 1 Peter 3:7 KJV

[69] Col. 3:19 KJV
[70] Eph. 5:25 KJV
[71] Psalm 1 KJV
[72] 1 Cor. 13:1 NIV
[73] 1 Cor. 13:2 NIV
[74] 1 Cor. 13:3 NIV
[75] 1 Cor. 13: 4 NIV
[76] 1 Cor. 13:5 NIV
[77] 1 Cor. 13:5 NIV
[78] 1 Cor. 13:6 NIV
[79] 1 Cor. 13:7 NIV
[80] 1 Cor. 13:13 NIV
[81] Gal. 1:6-12 KJV
[82] 2 Cor. 11:3-6, 12-15 KJV
[83] Matt. 16:19-21 NIV
[84] Eph. 6: 10-20 NIV
[85] James 1:22 NIV

Works Cited

Tozer, A. W. "This World: Playground or Battleground?" calvarypo.org/HANDS/0692.pdf

Yeats, William Butler. "The Second Coming." www.poetryfoundation.org/poems/43290/the-second-coming

Printed in Poland
by Amazon Fulfillment
Poland Sp. z o.o., Wrocław